SHOWDOWN

SHOWDOWN

•

Robert Stokesberry

AVALON BOOKS
NEW YORK

© Copyright 2004 by Robert Stokesberry
Library of Congress Catalog Card Number: 2004095205
ISBN 0-8034-9701-6
Published by Thomas Bouregy & Co., Inc.
160 Madison Avenue, New York, NY 10016

PRINTED IN THE UNITED STATES OF AMERICA
ON ACID-FREE PAPER
BY HADDON CRAFTSMEN, BLOOMSBURG, PENNSYLVANIA

Chapter One

For the past hundred miles the land had been flat and sere—true desert, the ground clean and sandy, dotted with scattered clumps of scrub brush and cactus—but now more mesquite, manzanilla and juniper began to show as the elevation climbed. Further ahead, ridges rose to form a range of hills, with the jagged edges of pine trees outlined against the horizon. The increasing green, the change in scenery after the barrenness of the desert, pleased Clay. He liked this land, although the high altitude and dryness rasped a bit at his throat and lungs. He knew that there was a town a few miles ahead—a town big enough to have a saloon. Hell, out here in the West, even a wide spot in the road usually managed to have something that passed for a saloon, even if it was only a simple lean-to.

The thought of going into a town made Clay hesitate. If it was a town big enough to have the kind of saloon he was looking for, it was probably big enough to have law officers. Clay was averse to putting himself in the path of any kind of law officer. However, he probably wasn't known in these parts; white settlement was too recent. It was only the discovery of gold that had brought people in at all, and there had not been much gold. From what he'd heard, a couple of hundred miles

1

back along the trail, the few larger strikes had played out quickly and now there were only small diggings—which meant even fewer people who might recognize him. He'd been checking his back trail for the past few days, and had not been able to discover anybody following. He was pretty sure of what was, or wasn't, behind him, but only vaguely sure of what might lie ahead.

Over the past couple of months he'd spent most of his time on the trail—had taken to the trail after all that trouble back in Wyoming, when a bounty hunter had tried to bring him in. Now, Clay wondered if there'd be a few people to talk to. Some human company might be nice, even if it was only the company of a talkative bartender.

Clay's horse sensed his interest, and broke into an easy trot. Clay let the horse carry him along, but that did not stop him from keeping a watchful eye on the landscape. There was movement off to the right, but it was just a couple of antelope, and they weren't moving as if anything or anyone had spooked them.

Clay was riding a few hundred yards away from the main trail. When he reached high ground, he checked the landscape ahead. About a mile away the main trail intersected with another, smaller trail that came in from the right. That other trail, where it headed to the left, ended at the town. The intersection would be the area to watch; the two trails looked as if they crossed somewhere down inside a little wash—a good place for an ambush.

He rode wide, approaching the intersection at an angle. When he was a few hundred yards away, he saw that a wagon was nearing the intersection, coming from a fold of land off to the right. There seemed to be three people in the wagon. Clay rode his horse into the cover of a patch of manzanilla. Not bothering to dismount, he reached behind him and slid a pair of powerful binoculars out of his saddlebags. He sat in the saddle for a moment, studying the wagon. With the aid of the glasses, he could see that there were indeed three people in the wagon, two women and a man.

The wagon disappeared into the little wash that led to the intersection. Clay rode out of his cover and headed slowly toward the intersection, intending to let the wagon clear the low spot before he turned toward the town. He figured that the wagon would probably be heading into town, and his plan was to follow along, just out of sight.

To his surprise, the wagon did not emerge from the wash. He waited, still no wagon. Clay, mildly curious, not too worried about a couple of women and one man, continued on toward the wash. He was about fifty yards away when he heard voices—several male voices and the voice of a woman, shouting.

Much more interested now, Clay approached the low spot, riding up the back side of the rise that led to it. As he rode, he slipped his Winchester from its saddle scabbard, and held it balanced across the pommel of his saddle.

From the volume of talk down inside the wash, he doubted anyone down there would be paying much attention to anything else. He heard a man laugh, loud and harsh, then the woman's voice rose again, her tone angry. "Jeffers," she was saying, "you let us pass, or—"

"Or what?" a male voice replied. "You gonna faint on me, you old bat?"

"Don't you talk to her that way!" another male voice called out. It sounded like the voice of a boy, or a very young man.

"Oh yeah?" the first man's voice replied. "You willin' to risk a bullet for it?"

"Jesus, Jeffers," another man said. "Why don't we just take them two women outta the wagon and show 'em a real good time?"

"Yeah, both of 'em look like they was made special for a little rollin' around on the ground."

Clay had heard enough. He urged his horse forward.

There was already a cartridge in the Winchester's chamber; he always rode with a round chambered. Now he cocked the hammer, holding down the trigger to keep the action from making any noise, then eased the trigger forward again, so that it engaged the hammer sear. As he rode over the top of the high ground, he saw three mounted men, sitting their horses just a few feet away from the wagon. One glance was enough to tell Clay that he was looking at gunslingers.

The wagon was halted in a patch of sand. Clay quickly scanned its three passengers, who were still seated, although one of the women was starting to stand on the wagon bed. She was a good-looking woman, perhaps forty years old. A younger woman was seated next to her, certainly no more than twenty years old. Clay took a moment to study the girl—thick, blond hair, large blue eyes, a lovely face, and lots of woman beneath a simple dress.

The man inside the wagon, a boy, couldn't be much more than fifteen or sixteen. A good looking boy, he stood up suddenly inside the wagon bed, his face flushed with anger. "Mr. Jeffers," he shouted, "you're a foul-mouthed good-for-nothing—" The boy bent, reaching for what looked like a shotgun that was lying on the floor of the wagon.

One of the men suddenly spurred his horse forward and in one quick motion slid a pistol out of the well-oiled holster on his right hip. Clay thought for a moment that the man was going to shoot the boy. Clay started to raise his rifle, but the horseman simply slammed the barrel of his pistol against the side of the boy's head.

Both women shouted—the girl's shout more of a scream, the older woman's voice angry, but frightened too. The boy fell half out of the wagon, blood showing on the side of his head. The riders fanned out a little more around the wagon. The man who'd done the pistol-whipping was now pointing his pistol down at the boy.

"You pull that trigger, and you're a dead man," Clay called out.

The tableau below him froze in place. The women were now both standing up in the wagon, their faces white with anger and fear, but Clay had most of his attention concentrated on the three horsemen. The one with the pistol looked back over his shoulder at Clay. He tried to bring the pistol around, but the barrel hung up in his horse's reins. The other two men twisted in their saddles, their hands drifting down towards the butts of their pistols. It looked like there wasn't going to be any way to avoid a fight.

One of the other two men decided to make his move. It was a fast move, so that Clay had to react just as quickly. Raising his Winchester to his shoulder, he shot the man through the body. The man had time to let out one loud squawk, then he fell over the side of his horse. By now Clay had spurred his own mount forward, hoping he would not have to shoot anyone else. If he ended up killing three men, not more than a few miles from town, he could kiss that beer goodbye.

He rode in among the two men who were still mounted and slammed the barrel of his rifle against the head of the man closest to him, knocking him out of the saddle. Almost in the same motion, he brought the muzzle of his rifle to bear on the man who'd hit the boy. The man had finally untangled the reins from around the barrel of his pistol, and was trying to point it at Clay. Clay thrust his rifle toward the man, so that the muzzle was no more than a yard from his chest. He worked the loading lever, chambering another cartridge. "You choose, Mister," Clay said, his voice soft, under control. "You choose whether or not you're gonna catch a bullet."

The man's gaze fastened on the Winchester's muzzle for a moment, then moved up toward Clay's eyes. He wished he hadn't. He found himself looking into the coldest pair of eyes he'd ever seen—eyes like chips of blue ice, eyes totally without expression.

He dropped his pistol. It thudded softly onto the sand. He

managed to hold his gaze locked with Clay's gaze for a moment, then he was forced to look away. "Mister," he muttered, "you done gone and bought yourself a peck o' trouble."

"Then maybe I should just go ahead and shoot you now," Clay said coldly.

"Hey, now hold on just a minute—" the man said weakly.

"No. Two seconds. And if you're not down from your horse by then . . ."

"Yeah, yeah—I'm gettin'," the man said hurriedly.

"Make sure you keep your hand away from the butt of that rifle."

The man swung down from the saddle, some of the fear going out of his eyes now that it appeared that he was going to live. The fear was slowly replaced by a look of intense hatred.

Clay swung down too, covering the man with his rifle as he moved over to the two men lying on the ground. Clay motioned the disarmed man aside, then, bending down, he jerked the pistol out of the holster of the man he'd hit with his rifle barrel and threw the pistol into a patch of brush.

The man who'd just been faced down bent over the man Clay had shot and rolled him over roughly. A loud groan indicated that the man was still alive. While all this was going on, Clay kept watch on the two women in the wagon, and on the boy, who'd slipped all the way down onto the ground, his hands pressed against his bloody scalp. You never knew where trouble might come from; with this many people around, better to stay alert.

Both women jumped down out of the wagon, and knelt by the boy. "Jimmy," the girl cried out. "Are you okay?"

"Yeah, I'm okay," the boy murmured.

The older woman took a quick look at his bloody head. "Just a cut," she said. "Can you get back up into the wagon?"

Jimmy nodded, winced and seemed to get dizzy—but with the womens' help, he managed to hoist himself aboard. Clay remembered the shotgun, but the older of the two women had remembered it, too. She took it out of the wagon, and aimed it at the three men on the ground. She cranked both hammers back and the man who'd hit Jimmy spun around and saw the shotgun leveled at him. He turned white. "Mrs. Johnson . . . you wouldn't. . . ."

"Jeffers, you piece of scum," she said, "after what you did to my boy, after what you said you wanted to do to my daughter and me . . ."

Her voice was so cold, so choked with half-suppressed fury, that Clay was certain she was going to shoot. Then she lowered the twin muzzles, but just a little, so that they were pointed at the lower legs of the man she'd called Jeffers. "Get back on your horse," she said. "You ride on out of here, and maybe you'll live."

Jeffers tore his eyes away from the cavernous black holes in the muzzle of the shotgun. He looked down at the man Clay had shot. "But Curly, here—he's hurt bad."

"So put him on his horse," the woman said. "Take him back to Duval, and tell Duval that—"

Clay could see that the woman was beginning to run down a little, that the rage was no longer enough to sustain her. She moved back toward the wagon. The girl put an arm around her, which made the muzzle of the shotgun waver, so that it panned over the three men on the ground. Jeffers looked up, and seeing the wavering shotgun, turned white again. "For God's sake, Mrs. Johnson, point that thing up in the air."

Jeffers and his friend were getting the wounded man up onto his feet. Clay saw that his bullet had passed through the man's right arm, then struck him in the body. A large patch of blood showed where the bullet had gone in. Clay doubted it had done too much damage. The way the arm was hanging, the bullet had hit and broken the upper arm bone, and had probably lost a lot of its force by the time it hit the man's body. For a moment, he thought of asking the women to put the man in the wagon, but he seemed to be moving well enough as Jeffers and the other man hoisted him onto his horse.

While they were intent on the wounded man, Clay went over to Jeffers's mount, and slipped Jeffers's Winchester out of its saddle scabbard. He did the same with the rifles of the other two men, and threw all three of the rifles into the wagon. "Hey, Mister, those are our rifles," the man Clay had cold-cocked said angrily, then decided to shut up.

Within a couple of minutes, all three men were mounted. They pulled the heads of their horses around and started to ride off. Jeffers rode just a few feet, and then he turned in the saddle, facing Clay. "Mister," he grated, his voice full of hatred. "I don't know who you are, but you're gonna be sorry!"

Now the woman spoke. "You going to sic Duval on him, Jeffers?" she asked, her voice taunting. "Or do you think you've got the guts to do something all on your own?"

"Lady," Jeffers snapped. "You got a big mouth."

The shotgun tracked toward him again. He'd ridden off a little ways, but was still close enough for the buckshot to turn him into hamburger. He started to open his mouth, then suddenly spurred his horse away. A moment later, all three of the men had disappeared up the wash. The wounded man was swaying a little in his saddle, but managed to hold his seat well enough.

Still, Clay did not completely relax until the woman had lowered both of the shotgun's big hammers.

Chapter Two

The woman laid the shotgun back inside the wagon bed, next to Jimmy, while the girl used a cloth to wipe some of the blood from the side of his head. Clay stood for a moment, looking along the trail, just in case the three men he'd run off might choose to return and renew the argument. The woman saw what he was doing, then said, "They won't be back. Jeffers is mean and dangerous, kind of like a coyote can be dangerous. He'll bite when your back is turned, but run fast when it looks like he might get hurt."

Clay nodded. He'd read Jeffers pretty much the same way. To Clay, any man who molested women had to be a coward. He walked over to his horse and took the reins, ready to mount. "Where are my manners?" the woman said. "I haven't thanked you for helping us. If you hadn't shown up, well . . . I can't say I really know what might have happened."

Clay looked up, past the woman, to find his eyes meeting those of the girl. He and the girl looked at one another for several seconds. At first, it appeared to Clay that she might blush and drop her gaze, but instead she smiled, her entire face lighting up. "Yes," she said, nodding, agreeing with her mother. She was a pretty girl.

"I suppose we'd better get into town," the woman said. "I want the doctor to look at Jimmy's head."

"Ah, Mom," the boy said. "It ain't nothin'." Then he blushed, remembering how scared he'd been when he'd seen Jeffers go for his pistol. He looked up at Clay, and wished he was like him. He remembered how cool Clay had been throughout the whole thing, how casually he'd shot Jeffers's companion out of his saddle.

Jimmy suddenly slipped over the side of the wagon, then went over to the patch of brush where Clay had thrown the pistol of the gunslinger. After a quick search, the boy found the pistol. He started to hold it out to Clay, but Clay shook his head. "Keep it," he said. "You earned it. Three against one, and you went for the shotgun."

The boy beamed with pleasure. At that moment, he would have done anything for Clay.

The boy's mother came up to Clay. "My name's Jessica," she said. "Jessica Johnson. That's my daughter Molly, and my son, Jimmy. We all owe you a great deal, Mister . . . ?"

"Parker," Clay replied. "Clay Parker." For just a moment, he'd considered falling back on another name he often called himself, Rankin, but one more glance at the girl had kept him from giving a name he might later have to retract. Her smile, still just as radiant, had grown a little more personal—which may have been why he said, a moment later, "Maybe it'd be a good idea if I rode along with you at least part of the way."

A quick, amused smile played across Jessica's face; she'd noticed the way Clay had been looking at her daughter. She felt a little tug of alarm, but immediately dismissed it. After all, this stranger had just done them a great service—and Molly was a grown woman now, more or less.

Molly was thinking the same thing. Now that the fear had gone, now that the danger was past, she'd been spending a little time studying the man who'd rescued them. She'd noticed right away that he was tall; he even looked tall sitting his horse. He had thick brown hair, and a mustache of the same color. She didn't normally like mustaches, but this one seemed to set off the whiteness of the man's teeth. It was mostly the stranger's eyes that intrigued her. Blue eyes—a friendly blue now, but she'd noticed that when he'd stared Jeffers down, those eyes had narrowed to icy slits. She shivered a little as she remembered, the shiver turning into a thrilling warmth deep down in the pit of her belly.

She turned her attention away while her mother accepted the stranger's offer of an escort. A minute later, Clay, having remounted, was riding alongside the wagon. Jessica drove with Molly sitting next to her and Jimmy in back, propped against some empty sacks while he examined the pistol he'd retrieved from the brush, turning it over and over in his hands.

When they'd gone about a mile, Clay remembered something Jessica had said about someone named Duval. He also remembered Jeffers's threat that Clay would be sorry. So he asked Jessica who Duval was.

"Henry Duval," she replied. "Our beloved sheriff. There isn't much devilment around these parts that doesn't start, in some way, with Henry Duval."

"Him and Hank Slade and his riders," Molly put in. "They're really just a bunch of bandits trying to pretend they're cowhands."

"You see," Jessica continued, "this is pretty wild country, and big. Jefferson County, that's where we are now, is really huge. There's lots of trouble—bandit gangs, rustlers—as much trouble as a place can have."

"That Slade bunch," Molly said. "They're the biggest gang, and with Henry Duval as sheriff, they do pretty much what they want."

Clay said nothing. It was an old story. In the West, particularly in an area like this, with a scattered population made up mostly of individuals who hated interference from the law, a crooked sheriff could get away with just about anything. Clay had met more than one crooked sheriff—something most people just put up with. No matter how crooked the sheriff, shooting a lawman usually brought big trouble.

"I don't know how any of us could survive out here, if it wasn't for the Kerson brothers," Molly said.

"Oh," Jessica replied. "They aren't much better."

"At least they don't encourage men like Jeffers to go around molesting women."

"Molly's just saying that 'cause she's sweet on Jack Kerson," Jimmy said. He'd seen the way Molly was shining up to Clay, and seen the way Clay had been looking back at her. He was jealous; Clay was his find. He saw that his remark had struck home. Molly was blushing furiously. "That isn't so!"

Seeing that Clay had once more been left wondering, Jessica said, "The Kerson brothers are town marshals. They control the town the way that Henry Duval and the Slade gang control the county."

"Not *quite* the same way," Molly said spiritedly. "They're not like them at all."

"Gamblers," Jessica replied. "And all those women that they, well . . ."

Molly looked like she wanted to reply to that, but she caught Clay looking at her. She finally blushed and looked away. Clay thought that perhaps she really was, as her brother had said, sweet on one of the town marshals. Too bad, because Clay was beginning to appreciate Molly more and more. She was not only lovely to look at, she also seemed to have spirit.

"There's kind of a war between Sheriff Duval and the Kerson brothers," Jessica said. "They're fighting each other for control of the county. The Kersons are fighting from inside the town, which is the county seat and the only real town for a couple of hundred miles and the Duval bunch are fighting from wherever they can. Molly is right, up to a point. The Kerson brothers are a little more decent, but they control the kind of activities in the town, that, well, that shouldn't be talked about in polite company. I never heard of them robbing and killing, the way the Duval bunch does. I mean, there's not actual proof that Duval and his cronies are doing all the things they're accused of doing, but nobody has much doubt about it. Nobody says much, of course. Not openly. Henry Duval has a long arm."

Once again Clay said nothing. It looked like he had stuck his nose into a power struggle for control of this huge chunk of land and for control, naturally, of whatever loose money was lying around for the taking. If he had any brains, he'd take the two women and the boy into town, then ride right out. However, each time he looked over at Molly, he wondered if it might not be interesting to stay in the area for just a little while. The way the girl kept looking at him . . .

The town was already in sight. It was a considerably larger place than Clay had expected. He could see several buildings of three or four stories, although most were just one or two stories. A few buildings were made of stone—and instead of just one dusty main street, or the usual rutted dirt tracks running past weathered board buildings, there were three streets running parallel through the town, with half a dozen cross streets. Clay estimated that possibly as many as three or four thousand people lived in the town, which would also be a center for the surrounding countryside. A real metropolis—which meant it would have its share of grief, because wherever people gathered there was bound to be some kind of trouble.

Jessica took the wagon straight into the center of town, down the dusty main street. She pulled the horses to a stop in front of a large general store. When she got down from the wagon, Molly did the same. Clay caught a glimpse of trim ankle as the girl's skirt rode up a little. He politely looked away, then noticed that a ghost of a smile was tugging at the girl's lips. She had seen where he was looking, and did not seem particularly disturbed.

Jimmy was starting to get down from the wagon too, somewhat gingerly. "I'd better get you over to Doc Jones's place," Jessica started to say to the boy. Then the sound of horses pounding down the street caused her to look up. "Oh-oh," she burst out. "I think trouble just rode in after us."

Clay looked where she was looking and saw Jeffers and his two companions riding up the street. The wounded man was still sitting his saddle, but looked extremely pale. Jeffers glanced in the direction of the wagon and the little group of people gathered around it. Clay swung down from his horse. Common sense said to keep mounted, so that he could simply spur away if trouble developed, but he didn't want to leave the Johnsons behind to face trouble alone. He remained standing close to his horse.

"There's Sheriff Duval," Molly said.

Clay looked down the street. Clay could see the glitter of a badge on the man's shirt, half-hidden by a black coat. The tail of the coat rode up over the butt of a revolver that the man wore on his right hip. An alert man, Clay decided. He'd heard something out of the ordinary, perhaps the sound of horses being ridden hard, and he had come out to investigate.

"Sheriff!" Jeffers sang out. "That son of a gun over there shot Curly!"

He was pointing toward Clay and the Johnsons. In the meantime, one of the other men was helping Curly out of the saddle. Curly almost fell, but managed to hang onto the saddle horn until he was able to plant both feet on the ground.

Jeffers was halfway to the sheriff by then, talking excitedly. From where he stood, Clay could hear Jeffers spinning a hair-raising tale of unprovoked attack against peaceful men.

The sheriff's eyes tracked onto Clay. He began to walk in Clay's direction, with Jeffers tagging along after him. *Oh-oh*, Clay thought. *I should have just kept on riding.*

The sheriff stopped a few yards away and studied Clay for a few seconds. While Clay did the same to the sheriff, who was of a little more than medium height, well-built, without

being heavy, and perhaps forty years old. There was something about his face that marred his looks. Not any particular facial feature, but rather something in his expression—
not exactly a coldness, but a look of calculation. It was the
kind of calculation that Clay had come to associate with
greed and ruthlessness.

"That's him!" Jeffers was pointing at Clay again, yelling
half into the sheriff's ear. "That's the man who shot Curly."

The sheriff looked straight at Clay. "Is that right?" he
asked. "Did you shoot that man?"

Clay was surprised. The sheriff's voice was surprisingly
high-pitched and thin, out of keeping with the way he
looked. It was not a pleasant voice. "Yes," Clay replied.
"I . . ."

"Then unbuckle that gun belt," the sheriff said. "You're
under arrest, Mister."

There had been no questions asked about what actually
happened, how the shooting might have come about. The
sheriff was simply taking the word of Jeffers, Duval was
looking straight at Clay, his face expressionless.

It appeared to Clay as if he was going to spend some time
in the local lock-up. For a minute he considered just getting
up on his horse and riding out of town, maybe pulling his
gun if the sheriff tried to stop him, but by now a crowd had
begun to gather. It would be idiocy to pull down on a lawman with a whole street full of people watching. Many of
the men who had gathered were armed. Probably some of
them would back the sheriff.

"This isn't right!" he heard Molly call out. "He was just
protecting us. Jeffers and those other two men—"

"What's going on here?" another voice cut in. It was a voice
that carried, a voice full of authority and self-confidence.

"Nothing that's any of your business, Kerson," the sheriff
replied. "This man shot Curly and I'm arresting him."

Clay looked over at the man who'd called out. He was a
big man, tall and lean, but not thin. He, too, had a badge

pinned to the front of his shirt—not a star, like the sheriff's badge, but the rounded shield of a marshal, or town police-man. "Duval," the man snapped, "everything that happens in this town is my business. If anybody is going to get arrest-ed, then I'm gonna be the one doin' the arresting."

"It's still none of your business, Kerson," the sheriff replied. "The shooting took place outside the city limits, so it's my concern."

The two lawmen stood facing one another, only a few yards apart. It was clear they did not care much for each other. Clay figured that the newcomer had to be the town marshal Jessica had told him about, and that the obvious ten-sion between the two men had its roots in the struggle for power that she had described. Clay remembered that Jessica had mentioned more than one Kerson, a group of brothers. Clay wondered if this was the one that Molly was supposed to be sweet on. He could understand why, while there was something in the big man's face that Clay didn't feel totally at ease with, he was definitely an improvement over Sheriff Duval.

By now, Molly was pushing nearer, with Jessica just a step behind. "Marshal," Molly said, pointing at Clay, "He helped us. Jeffers, and those two skunks with him, stopped us out on the trail. They hit my brother over the head, then said that they were going to . . . that they were going to do things to my mother and me."

A muttering rose from the crowd. "That sounds like somethin' Jeffers would do, all right," one man said loudly. "By God, any man who'd bother a woman . . ."

There was more muttering from the crowd. Suddenly, Jeffers was looking worried. Jessica had now stepped up beside her daughter. Marshal Kerson motioned to her. "Is that right, Mrs. Johnson?" he asked.

"Yes. Just like Molly told it. If it hadn't been for this stranger . . . well, he told Jeffers and his cronies to let us alone. Then they pulled their guns, and he shot that one."

She was pointing at Curly, who was now slumped in a chair up on the boardwalk. "He could have shot the other two," Jessica continued, "but he just took away their guns, and told them to leave. Then he escorted us into town, in case there was any more trouble." She turned to point at Jeffers. "When men like that are permitted to run around loose . . ." she said tightly. "When women and children aren't safe out of doors . . ."

Clay saw Jimmy's face color when his mother used the word "children." By now there were angry cries from the crowd. "Oughta string 'em up," one man said. "Molestin' decent women . . ."

"There won't be no stringing up anybody," the sheriff snapped.

"Not when he's one of your pet dogs," Marshal Kerson said, grinning at the sheriff. Somebody in the crowd laughed. Kerson looked at Jessica questioningly, then pointed toward Jeffers and his two cronies. "You want me press charges against 'em, Ma'am?"

"No, Marshal," Jessica replied, after a moment's hesitation. She looked in the direction of the wounded man. "I suppose they've been punished enough."

"Molly?" the marshal asked.

"I'll go along with whatever my mother says, Jack."

Well, well, Clay thought. *Molly, Jack. First names. Maybe Billy was right about his sister and the marshal.* He felt a slight tug of jealousy. *Stupid*, he said to himself. He didn't really even know the girl, but he realized that he'd like to have a chance to get to know her better.

The marshal and the sheriff were facing one another like two dogs trying to decide whether or not to fight. Clay looked down the street and saw two hard-looking men standing in the doorway of the sheriff's office. They, too, had stars pinned to their shirts—deputies. Coming from the other direction Clay saw two other men with marshals' badges. Their resemblance to Jack Kerson indicated that they must be the other Kerson brothers.

Darn . . . a confrontation between lawmen, with himself standing smack dab in the middle. Fortunately, the crowd was angry over the tale of two women being molested. One thing a man did not dare do in the West was bother decent women, even outlaws had been known to kill other outlaws for molesting women.

Marshal Kerson made up his mind. He turned toward Jeffers, then pointed at Curly. "Take that sorry son of a snake over to Doc's and get him patched up."

Jeffers, grateful to have a chance to leave, had turned part way around when Kerson took him by the upper arm and spun him so that they were face to face. Kerson moved very close to Jeffers, looked him in the eye, then said softly, "Jeffers, if I ever hear of you bothering Molly and her mother again—or any of her family—if I hear anything like that . . . I'm gonna kill you, Jeffers. I'll shoot you down like the dog you are."

Jeffers tried to meet the marshal's gaze, failed, and looked down. Kerson stepped even closer. "Did you hear me, Jeffers?" he asked. "Did you hear what I just said?"

Jeffers nodded dumbly.

"'Cause it's the only warning you're gonna get," Kerson hissed. Then he turned around to face the sheriff. "That goes for any of your bunch, Duval," he said, loud enough for everyone to hear.

It could have developed into an open fight, but the crowd was still with the Johnson family, and as an extension of that, with Kerson—although Clay saw several members of the crowd looking toward Kerson with little fondness.

"Don't push it, Kerson," the sheriff said. He turned and started to walk away. After a few paces he stopped, then turned to face Clay. "I'll remember you, Mister," he said, his high, thin voice taught with anger. "If you know what's good for you, you'll stay out of trouble. Or better yet, ride on out of this county while you still have the chance."

Clay met the sheriff's gaze steadily. The two men stared

at one another for several long seconds. Clay was beginning to grow angry. His eyes had narrowed down again. It was the sheriff who looked away first, but in the seconds before the sheriff's gaze shifted, Clay could read in the other man's eyes that he'd made a deadly enemy.

Chapter Three

As soon as the sheriff was out of sight, the general mood relaxed. Clay noticed that Jeffers could no longer be seen, nor could either of the two men who had been with him. No doubt they'd taken the wounded man to the doctor. Clay was worried. What if the man died?

Meanwhile, Jessica, Molly, and Jimmy had gone into the big general store. Clay thought of getting on his horse and simply riding away, but he'd hate to let Duval think he'd driven him out of town, which might seem true if he left. Only an idiot hung around where there was bound to be trouble. Suddenly, Clay was aware that someone was coming up on his left side. Instinctively his hand drifted down toward the butt of his revolver. "No need for that," Kerson said. "We don't do Duval's dirty work. Or was that just habit?"

Kerson was smiling when he asked the question, but Clay could sense that the lawman in Kerson had surfaced. "It's been that kind of day," Clay replied.

"Yeah, I guess so. Good work, puttin' a slug in Curly. I wish you'd been able to put one in Jeffers, too."

"Seems like somebody'll have to do it eventually," Clay said. "He ain't easy to like."

The marshal burst out laughing. He turned toward his

brothers. "Hey—Luke, Mark. Our friend here just said that Jeffers ain't easy to like."

The other two men gave short barking laughs. Neither seemed to be the type who'd be liable to laugh as fully as their brother. They moved closer. The marshal turned back toward Clay. "I'm Jack Kerson," he said. "And these are my brothers, Luke and Mark." He laughed again. "Our folks were big bible thumpers. If there'd been another of us, I'm sure they'd have named him Matthew."

When he stuck out his hand, Clay knew that he was actually asking for a name. Once again, Clay was tempted to fall back on Rankin, but just then Jimmy came out of the store, carrying a sack of flour. "Parker," Clay said. "Clay Parker."

Fortunately, the name did not appear to mean anything to Kerson. He and Clay shook hands, both men aware of the other's strong grip. "I'm afraid you've stepped right into the middle of some local trouble," Kerson said. "That slippery son of a gun, Duval . . ."

"Mrs. Johnson mentioned a few things," Clay replied. "Duval lived up to her description."

"Well, I'll add to that description. You made a real bad enemy when you took on some of the coyotes that run with him. He hates the whole Johnson family too."

"Why? What could he have against two women and a boy?"

"There's Tom Johnson too—not that any of them have ever done anything to Duval. It's simply that they won't cowtow to him. Tom Johnson stood up to him, and the two women don't make any secret of how they feel about Duval. As far as they're concerned, he's something that stuck to the bottom of their shoes."

"Would he hurt them?"

Kerson shrugged, then glanced over at his brothers. "Not while we're around, but I kind of wonder if maybe Duval didn't sic those three yahoos onto 'em. Found out they were on their way into town, and . . . or just told 'em to give 'em a hard time if they got a chance. Thanks you, Parker. I'm much obliged to you."

Clay let that one pass—*much obliged*—as if Kerson held some kind of proprietary interest in the Johnsons, which probably meant Molly. Although, despite what Jimmy had said, he hadn't noticed any girlish fainting spells while Molly had been around the marshal. Besides, Kerson didn't look like the kind of man who'd get out of control over a woman. Despite his surface heartiness, Clay detected a streak of single-minded ambition in Kerson. It was an ambition that was more likely to be pointed in the direction of money and power than hearth and home.

It wasn't any of Clay's business. He was tired of looking at badges and stars pinned on the shirts of hard, ambitious men. It was time to think about hitting the trail. He spotted Molly and her mother coming out of the store, lugging packages. He followed the Kerson brothers as they rushed to help the two women load their goods into the wagon. Clay noticed how the marshal contrived to brush against Molly while they were working. Molly started to smile, then noticed that Clay was watching, and the smile grew somewhat tentative.

Kerson may have noticed. He moved away from Molly and turned to Jessica. "I don't think you ought to ride back to your place alone," he said. Clay wondered if he was about to offer to ride along, but Kerson added, "Me and my brothers have to stay in town, keep an eye on Jeffers and a few other reptiles. I think I heard Sam Jones and his sons say they were heading out this afternoon. They'd be riding in the same direction as you. Should I ask them?"

"Well, I don't want to put anybody out, Marshal, but it might be a good idea. What happened today was pretty upsetting. I didn't think they'd ever try anything like that, not in broad daylight."

"It won't get any better, not with the four of you living out there alone. You really ought to sell out and move into town."

Jessica ruefully shook her head. "Tom would never sell until he's made his strike. He's absolutely sure he's going to hit big any day."

While Clay was trying to make sense out of that, Kerson walked over to a group of men. He engaged three of them in conversation, while he pointed back toward Jessica. Clay figured it was probably Sam Jones and his sons.

Meanwhile, Jessica was asking Molly to go back into the store to get the last of their purchases. On impulse, Clay followed her inside to help her carry her purchases—he told himself, although he knew it was the way she'd looked at him before turning to walk inside that made him follow. It was a look subtly different from the way she'd looked at Kerson. Or, once again, so Clay told himself.

The interior of the store was dim and cluttered, with goods stacked up several feet high in places. He found Molly on the far side of some tall shelves, putting cans of fruit into a shopping basket. The basket already looked heavy; it sagged from her hand. Clay took it from her. "Thank you, Mr. Parker," she said.

"Call me Clay," he said.

"Well, thank you, Clay. And I don't mean for holding my basket. I was so scared out there."

For a moment he wondered if she was playing some kind of game. He remembered her as having shown little outright panic when faced with Jeffers and his companions. Instead, she'd displayed mostly anger and courage. Then he realized that she was not pretending. She was standing very close to him, and he could see a slight tremor on her lower lip. Perhaps she was suffering a delayed reaction to the danger. He suddenly felt a great tenderness toward her, especially when he looked into those huge blue eyes, a little misty now from unshed tears. "I thought they were going to . . ." she started to say.

Then suddenly she was even closer. His hand instinctively rose to touch her cheek. Her skin felt like silk. She suddenly pressed herself against him, her arms going around him, holding on for a moment. Her cheek brushed his. Then he felt her lips, one quick kiss against his cheek—a wonderful sensation, but not half as wonderful as the feel of her body against his, the soft firmness of a woman pressing against him, the sweet smell of her hair. It lasted only a moment, and then she stepped back, flushed, and apparently a little confused by what she had just done. Then there was the sound of Jessica calling from outside, Molly . . . ?"

"I . . . I had better go," the girl said. She turned and headed for the door, then stopped just a few feet away. "Do you think you could come out and visit us some day?" she asked. "Please?"

She walked through the door onto the boardwalk. Clay stood rooted to the spot, watching her go. Then he realized that the basket was still hanging heavily in his hand.

He followed the girl outside. She was already seated inside the wagon. Clay put the basket down beside her. He was aware of Jessica, looking at him and back to Molly. Clay noticed that the girl's face was still flushed. One more questioning glance at Clay from Jessica, and then the Joneses, father and sons, rode up. A moment later the wagon was heading down the street, with the Jones men flanking it. For just a moment Molly looked back at Clay and gave him a small, secret smile. Even after the wagon had turned a corner and disappeared from view, Clay found himself remembering how huge the girl's eyes had looked, how lovely her face had been, so close to his own inside the store. There was an even stronger memory of how her body had felt against his own.

"You're in big trouble, Parker," he muttered to himself.

Chapter Four

Clay had originally headed toward town to wet his whistle, and his mouth was still dry as a rattlesnake's burrow. Fortunately, he was standing right in front of a saloon, and it was the biggest building in this part of town. In addition, the mob of lawmen that had been littering the street had disappeared—the sheriff and the Kerson brothers.

What he should do is get on his horse, ride out of town, and not come back. He'd managed to attract the attention of the law. So far, no one had shown any indication of knowing who he was, although there had been that one quick look of appraisal from Jack Kerson. One glimpse of the wanted poster and all that could change—if the poster had made it out this far, but probably not.

Clay's throat was getting dryer by the second, so he hitched his horse to the rail in front of the saloon. He hesitated for a few moments, tempted to slip his two rifles from their saddle scabbards and take them inside. He did not like being more than a few feet from the rifles.

Finally deciding that it might be stretching things a little to haul the rifles into the saloon, he stepped up onto the boardwalk and headed toward the saloon's swinging doors.

He had his pistol and a big bowie knife in its sheath at the left side of his waist.

By habit, as soon as he'd stepped into the dim interior of the saloon he moved to one side, his back to the wall, so that he would not be silhouetted against the outside light while his eyes were adjusting to the gloom. However, it wasn't all that dark inside. There was a chandelier hanging from the ceiling in the middle of the room—a dusty chandelier with parts missing and only half the candles lit, but still a chandelier. Also, with windows along two of the walls, a fair amount of daylight was entering.

"Parker," he heard a voice call out. He looked in the direction from which the voice had come, and saw Jack Kerson sitting with a couple of other men at a card table near the back of the saloon. The glance that took in Kerson took in the rest of the room. There were half a dozen men scattered at other tables, and three men standing at the bar. Nobody but Kerson was looking in his direction. Clay was aware that Kerson had noted his move, the way he'd slipped to the side of the doorway; a slight smile tugged at Kerson's lips. A smile of approval?

"Care to join the game?" Kerson asked, nodding his head toward an empty chair at his table.

"Could be," Clay replied, "just as soon as I take care of some unfinished business."

At that, every man turned to look at Clay, wondering if he might be that unfinished business. *A jumpy town*, Clay thought. The tension eased considerably when he walked up to the bar, ordered a beer, then downed half of it in one long draft. He sighed, feeling the bubbles exploding in his throat.

Kerson's voice again: "Invitation's still open."

Clay turned back to the bartender. "Draw me another one," he said, while he drained the rest of his first beer. The second beer thudded down onto the scarred, wet, bar top. Instead of drinking, Clay picked up the stein and carried it over to Kerson's table.

There were two other men at the table. One looked like a miner or workman. The other man was fairly well dressed, he had the appearance of a banker, a man of business.

As soon as he sat down, Clay realized he was in a fairly high-stakes game—well, in light of his meager resources. Despite his dusty, ragged clothes, the man who looked like a miner had a couple of small piles of gold nuggets in front of him, along with a fair-sized stack of poker chips. Being new to the game, Clay did not know if the man had won the chips, or bought them with his gold. The banker had plenty of chips, but also a glum expression that suggested to Clay that he had started with a lot more.

Clay pulled out a hundred dollars. A velvet lined box full of chips and decks of cards lay on the table top near Kerson's right hand. He took Clay's hundred dollars and counted out a stack of chips, which he pushed in front of Clay. Kerson was clearly running the game. Clay had seen it many times before, the local lawman running various gambling games in the local saloons. It was a way for a marshal or sheriff to supplement his meager salary, and a way for saloon owners to get legal protection for their establishments.

Clay found himself forced to play conservatively. Even so, his stack of chips began to slowly diminish, most of it ending up in front of Jack Kerson. A good chunk of the miner's chips, and an even greater number of the banker's, moved in the same direction. It was not that Kerson was such a great poker player; it was his manner as he played. His cold, direct gaze pinned down the other players, as if daring them to show a better hand than his own—a cold, though not overt, intimidation.

Clay forced himself to buckle down. For a while he held even, then began to draw ahead. Then it came—the big hand, the big pot. The betting climbed, each man playing his cards hard. With each round of betting the pot grew. The banker, sweating, laid his billfold on the table, took out a rather thin sheaf of money, and bought more chips from

Kerson. The way he pulled out that sheaf of bills told Clay that the banker was growing desperate. Clay wondered if the man was playing with bank depositors' money—if he actually was a banker. He smelled like a banker. To Clay, bankers had their own unique smell.

The miner stayed with the betting for one more round, then dropped out. The bet came around to Clay. Most of his chips were already out on the table. Without looking at the cards, he considered his hand. A Jack-high full house. They were playing five card draw, and while his hand was good, it was vulnerable, considering the game.

Clay sensed this would be the final betting round, and it was time to read faces. There was no way to read Jack Kerson's face, because there was nothing there but a disinterested granite stare. The banker, on the other hand, was sweating even more, his eyes full of a suicidal blend of fear and hope.

Although most of his attention was focused on the game, Clay had been aware, for some time, of three men standing at the bar. They were the kind of men he liked to keep an eye on; rough looking men, heavily armed, much the same as the men who'd harassed the Johnsons out on the trail. They'd been watching the game intently, muttering amongst themselves. "Looks like we got another one of them . . ." he heard one man say. Clay did not have time to try and figure out what that meant; he had to decide whether to fold or bet.

Clay decided to stay with his cards. He pushed in almost half of his remaining chips. The bet was now around to Kerson. His hand dropped to the chips in front of him, which were most of the chips on the table. Then he pulled his hand back. "I fold," he said evenly, fanning his cards face down onto the table top.

Clay was aware of a low chuckle from one of the men at the bar. He thought he heard one of them say: "A set-up."

Clay glanced up and saw that the man was staring at Kerson. The marshal glanced at the man. There was a moment of eye contact, then the man at the bar looked away. Kerson's face was still unreadable, bleak.

The game was now between Clay and the banker. The banker looked at Clay intently for a moment, then his eyes darted away. For a moment, Clay thought he was going to fold but, jerkily, the banker's right hand pushed out a pile of chips. "I'll meet your thirty and raise you forty more," he said, his voice breathy, strained.

That was all the money Clay had left. He was tempted to fold, but he pushed out four, ten dollar chips.

He could tell that the banker had hoped he'd fold; he was trying to buy the pot. A moment's hesitation, then the banker laid out his cards. A ten-high full house. Clay sat unmoving for a moment, watching hope blossom on the banker's sweaty, flushed face. Then Clay fanned out his own cards, face up. The banker's eyes moved over the cards, moved away, then moved back. One last facial tick, then, without a word, he picked up the few chips he had left, and walked away from the table.

Clay raked in his chips, then shoved them over to the marshal. "Like to cash in," he said.

Kerson nodded, and began to count out a combination of gold coins and bank notes. The man at the bar, the one who'd been making most of the comments, spoke up again, this time more loudly than before. "Like I said, boys . . . a set-up. The dealer's got himself a new shill."

Clay was too busy counting his windfall to react, then a wave of anger spread through him. His attention moved away from the money and swung onto the man at the bar, who met his gaze for a moment. Uncomfortable with what he read in Clay's eyes, the man quickly looked away.

Clay started to stand up, but Kerson put out a restraining hand. "Uh-uh," he said, his voice flat. "This hasn't got anything to do with you. There's a history here . . ."

The marshal stood up, a slow smooth motion that had him on his feet before anyone else was aware he was about to move. In two steps he was standing in front of the man at the bar, facing him directly. Clay was surprised; Kerson wasn't watching the other two men, who now moved around behind the marshal. Clay would not have expected him to be that careless.

"Sprote," Kerson said to the man in front of him, "your big mouth is going to buy you a hole in the ground."

Sprote grinned. "What's the matter, Kerson?" Sprote asked. "Too close to the truth? You win too much to be playing on the square . . ."

Clay knew that something had to happen now. He guessed that a lot of Kerson's income came from these card games. If he let a man like Sprote get away with suggesting he cheated, he might as well fold his tent and leave.

Kerson's move, when it came, was simple. He took half a step forward and stomped down on Sprote's left foot, and at the same time he drew his pistol. It was not a particularly fast draw, but perfectly timed, while all of Sprote's attention was on his foot. Sprote finally clawed for his own pistol, but Kerson simply reached out and seized Sprote's arm, pinning it in place. Then his own pistol swept out to the side, the barrel smashing against the side of Sprote's head, the front sight digging a groove across Sprote's forehead.

Sprote uttered something between a grunt and a shout. He staggered a little, blood pouring down his face. He was still struggling to free his right arm from Kerson's grip; he had hold of the butt of his pistol, but couldn't free it from the holster. Kerson raised his own pistol, rested the muzzle against the bridge of Sprote's nose, and cranked back the hammer. Sprote froze, his eyes crossing a little as he tried to stare at the gun muzzle pressing against his face. A slight smile tugged at Kerson's lips.

He's paying too much attention to Sprote, Clay thought, *and not enough to the two other men . . . if he's aware of them at all*. One had now moved completely around behind the marshal. The man's hand drifted down toward the butt of his pistol, his eyes full of hatred as he glared at the back of Kerson's head. Clay had little doubt that the man was about to shoot Kerson in the back. Clay stood up suddenly, and came right behind the man who was behind the marshal. Clay's pistol seemed to grow out of his right hand; no one there was aware of him actually drawing it, he had moved so smoothly. Clay placed his pistol against the back of the man's neck. It had grown very quiet inside the saloon. The sound of the pistol's hammer clicking back seemed very loud. The man behind Kerson froze.

"Your choice, friend," Clay said, almost lazily.

The man continued to stand very stiffly for a couple of seconds, then relaxed. "Sure," he muttered. "No need to . . ." His hands moved out to the side, away from his body, away from the butt of his pistol.

The third man was standing just a few feet away; Clay was able to look straight at him over the shoulder of the man in front of him. Clay pinned the man's gaze, which wavered, then fell away.

It was then, looking up, that Clay's gaze met another pair of eyes . . . Jack Kerson's, in the big mirror behind the bar. Clay realized that Kerson must have been watching the action behind him all the time, had never been unaware of the man moving around behind him, had been aware of every movement in the bar.

Clay looked up at the mirror again and met Kerson's eyes, baffled for a moment to see a look of disappointment in those eyes. Then Clay understood. The marshal had not meant for it to end this way. He had meant for there to be a more violent, a more permanent, ending. He had, in fact, set the whole thing up.

By the time Kerson turned away from the bar, his eyes had returned to their normal state of giving away very little at all. Sprote, meanwhile, was still sagging against the bar, his shirt red with the blood that coursed down from the cut Kerson's pistol barrel had left on his head. Now that the immediate danger of gunplay was past, the men with Sprote were growing bolder. "Didn't have no call, Marshal," the one closest to the bar said, "pistol-whippin' Sprote that way."

Kerson looked at the man for a moment, his eyes growing cold again. "Listen, you back-shooting scum, get out of here. The next time you try getting around behind me with a gun, I'll kill you where you stand."

The man held his ground for a moment, then, as Kerson took a half-step forward, the third man, the one Clay had pulled down on, moved over to Sprote and took him by the shoulder. "Let it lie, Tom," he said.

He glanced over at Kerson, who did not bother to look back. "Let it lie . . . for now," he added under his breath.

Once again, Kerson did not bother to take notice. The two men guided a staggering Sprote out through the swinging doors.

Kerson turned, walked back to the card table and sat down. He looked up at Clay. "Never finished cashing you in," he said. He motioned for Clay to sit opposite him. A few of Clay's chips were still sitting on the table. Kerson meticulously counted them, then just as meticulously counted out more money, which he pushed toward Clay.

When he looked back up at Clay his face was pleasant, with no sign at all that anything out of the ordinary had taken place. "They're some of the scum who hang around Duval," he said abruptly. "They have more guts than brains. I gotta admit, they took me just a little by surprise. I never figured they'd try anything that openly, particularly not in here. They probably saw that Mark and Luke weren't around. I'm glad you were here to watch my back, Parker."

Clay said nothing. He remembered that half-disappointed look in Kerson's eyes after the fight had fizzled out. "On the other hand," Kerson immediately added, almost as if he had been reading Clay's thoughts, "It might have been simpler to just . . ."

He let the thought die. "Whichever way, Parker, I owe you."

Clay shrugged. Kerson looked at him for a long moment. "You figuring on sticking around for a while?"

Clay almost shrugged again. *Sticking around?* He should have been on his way long ago but then, there was Molly. He'd like to see her at least one more time. "Is there a hotel in town?" he heard himself asking.

Kerson smiled broadly. "Just happen to know of a really fine place," he replied, grinning. Clay wondered what was tickling the man.

Kerson was already getting to his feet. "Put that loot away, and I'll take you right over."

Clay shrugged, this time a shrug of acceptance. After stuffing the money into his pockets, he followed Kerson out into the street. The marshal turned down an alley. Puzzled, Clay continued to follow. The alley led into a little back street, a cul-de-sac. Dominating one end of the cul-de-sac was a small three story building. No sign outside said "Hotel," but Kerson walked up onto the porch and without ringing the bell, opened the door, stood aside, and motioned for Clay to enter.

Caution made Clay hesitate before going inside, casting quick looks to the left and right. Then he was standing inside what did indeed look like the lobby of a small hotel—quite a nice lobby, with a clerk sitting behind a well-polished hardwood counter. Behind the clerk were the usual pigeon holes for mail or keys. Only two or three had anything in them. The clerk was looking inquiringly at Kerson. "Marshal?" he asked politely.

"Is the upstairs back room still empty?" Kerson asked.

"Sure, Marshal."

Kerson nodded his head toward Clay. "Mr. Parker, here, will be using it for a while."

The clerk nodded, reached under the counter and came up with a ring of keys. After working one off the ring, he handed it, not to Clay, but to Kerson, who proceeded to hold it out to Clay.

"Hey, now wait a minute," Clay protested. "I'm not even sure I can afford . . ."

"Anybody mention money yet?" Kerson replied.

Clay looked at him coolly. "That isn't the way I work."

Kerson nodded. "Didn't figure it was but you do have all that money you won off the banker. Let's say fifty cents a day."

So the card player had indeed been a banker. Clay looked up at Kerson questioningly when he realized it was the marshal who had made the offer, and not the clerk.

"Yeah," Kerson said. "I own the place. Well, me and Luke and Mark. We've got a few investments scattered around town."

And you want me to be one of them? Clay wondered, then immediately pushed the thought aside. Maybe it wasn't meant that way at all. Maybe Kerson was simply the good-natured, friendly man he seemed . . . despite what Clay had seen in his eyes in that one unguarded moment in the saloon.

Besides, there was a comfortable feeling about this little hotel. It had been a while since he'd had a place besides the hard ground for a bed. "Sounds okay to me," he finally replied.

Kerson gave a big grin then turned toward the clerk. "Send somebody over to the hitching rack in front of the saloon to collect Mr. Parker's horse and gear. It's a big bay, with two rifles in saddle scabbards, one of 'em a Sharps."

He turned toward Clay. "The hotel has its own stable just behind the rear door. Your horse'll be there."

Clay nodded. Kerson didn't miss much; he had already noticed the two rifles and the color of his horse. What else had he noticed? Clay decided to let it ride. Kerson was heading toward the door. "See you in the saloon later?" he asked.

"Could be," was all Clay replied as Kerson went out into

the street. Kerson was already determining enough of his behavior.

The clerk directed him toward the stairs. A few minutes later, Clay was unlocking the door of his room. He stepped inside. *A nice room*, he decided. It was worth considerably more than fifty cents a day. There was a big bed, a huge armoire, a chest of drawers, and a commode holding a basin and water pitcher. A large oriental rug covered the center of the well-polished floor. There was a tall oil lamp in one corner.

Clay heard the sound of footsteps coming up the stairs and approaching his door. He slipped to the side of the doorway, drew his pistol and held it down by his leg. There was a light rapping at the door. "Your gear, Mister?" a young male voice called out. Clay opened the door a crack and saw a boy of maybe fifteen, who did indeed look like a hostler, with Clay's saddlebags draped over one shoulder. He was carrying both rifles. A quick look down the short hallway showed Clay that there was no one behind the boy. He slipped his pistol back into its holster and reached out to take the rifles. "I figured you'd want the rifles first," the boy said.

"You figured right."

Smart kid. Or was this simply the kind of town where a kid grew up thinking that way? Clay gave the boy fifty cents. "I'll bring your bedroll up right away," the boy said, his eyes shining as he fingered the half dollar.

"Wait a minute," Clay said as the boy started out the door. "Is there any place in town where a man can take a bath?"

"Why, yessir," the boy replied, as if surprised that such a question needed to be asked. "There's a bathroom just down at the end of the hall. I'll ask Mr. Cutts, that's the desk manager, to send up some hot water."

My, my, Clay thought after the boy had gone. *A bathroom on the top floor. Quite a fancy little place for fifty cents a day.*

*   *   *

After his bath, Clay changed into his spare trousers and shirt, both a bit wrinkled, but which felt good after the dirt-stiffened clothes he'd been wearing for the past few days. The comfort of the room seduced him. He lay down on the bed, intending to rest for a few minutes, and fell asleep. When he finally awoke, the window was dark. Having no idea of how long he'd slept. Clay got up, lit the oil lamp after a bit of fumbling, then looked at his watch. It was ten o'clock.

He wasn't at all sleepy after his nap. He got up, strapped on his gun belt, and headed out the door.

His first impulse was to take up Kerson's invitation, and visit the saloon. Then he decided it might be time to take a look at his surroundings—in this case, the hotel—get to know the various turnings of the halls and check the exits in case he needed a quick way out.

Walking through the upper floors, Clay did not see another person. Finally, from a second floor window, he found himself looking down at a one-story wing, stretching away toward a back street. He saw soft light pouring from a couple of windows, and thought he heard the sound of a piano. What was all that about?

Going downstairs to the lobby, Clay looked in the direction of where that wing should be. It was painted the same dark color as the paneled walls, so it was a minute before he noticed a door set flush into one of the walls, obscured by the desk clerk's counter.

A sound came from behind him. Clay spun, his hand moving toward the butt of his pistol. The desk clerk, just coming in through the front entrance, involuntarily moved back a step. Clay let his hands hang loose at his sides. His gaze moved toward the half-hidden door. The clerk noticed, and now spoke. "Uh . . . the marshal said that if you showed any interest, I was to show you the private bar."

Private bar? Clay was sure he could hear the muffled sound of a piano again, coming from behind the door. The clerk moved behind the counter. Clay watched him yank on a cord, some kind of bell-pull. A moment later Clay heard the sound of a well-oiled lock being turned. The heavy door swung open. A man of about forty, wearing a formal suit, stood framed in the opening. He looked inquisitively from the clerk to Clay. The clerk motioned toward Clay. "A friend of the marshal's," he said. The man's face lit up. "Well, sir, any friend of Kerson . . ."

Now that the door was open, the sound of the piano was much louder. Looking past the man in the doorway, Clay saw a young woman sitting at a piano, playing a popular tune. Clay moved closer to the door and saw that the room had several tables and a short mahogany bar.

A man sat at the bar, nursing a drink. He was well dressed. *Looks like one of the town fathers*, Clay thought. The man in the doorway smiled at the look of confusion on Clay's face. "Very, very private," he said. "Will you come in, sir?"

Well, my God, Clay thought, *and all this for fifty cents a day*. He stepped inside and sat at one of the tables. The man who had answered the door moved around to stand behind the bar. Clay motioned to him. "A whiskey," he said. The drink came quickly. There was only himself and the man at the bar, besides the piano player. Clay wondered if the place made a profit. He suspected that only the people the marshal wanted to impress were welcomed here, and apparently Clay was one of those.

After sipping his whiskey for a while, he began to pay attention to the girl playing the piano. She played quite well. She was not the most beautiful girl Clay had ever seen, but she had about her an air of such self-possession, of calm, of such quiet loveliness, that Clay was drawn to her. She saw him looking at her, and smiled. It was not at all coquettish; just a friendly smile. Emboldened, Clay moved to a table next to the piano.

He and the girl began to talk in between tunes; he learned

that her name was Sarah. She was of medium height, and slim, but with a pleasing collection of curves. Her hair was dark, almost black. Her skin was creamy and dusky. She had large dark eyes and full lips. She seemed to exhibit both sensuality and innocence. Her obvious physical appeal was accompanied by flashes of wit and humor that suggested considerable intelligence.

When the man at the bar left, there was no one to play for except Clay. So when he showed an inclination to talk, she complied. They moved to a table in a corner of the room, and engaged in a slow-paced conversation. Sarah was very easy to talk to—and that seemed to be what she was here for, not just the piano playing, but as female company. She was not a bar girl; obviously she was of a quality much higher that that. Clay had not had an opportunity to talk to an intelligent, independent woman for a long time, and he was grateful for the opportunity.

Sarah told just enough of her story to inform, while holding enough back to maintain an aura of mystery. The story itself was not so very different from others he'd heard in similar settings, a girl brought up in a fairly prosperous, bible-thumping household—until Daddy, noticing how his little girl was flowering, began to let his hands roam. When Sarah, horrified, angrily rebuffed him, her father launched into the usual scripture-spouting hypocrite's condemnation of her as an intolerable temptation put before him by the devil.

Sarah refused to retreat into a cowed shell. Instead, one night she took the little bit of money her dead mother had left her and simply left home.

The money didn't last long. She had to work. For a while, she was a school teacher for a small town—she'd had considerable education, but trying to tame rambunctious frontier youths was more than she was willing to take on. She played the piano in a large saloon for a while, but found herself fighting off advances from some very rough men. It was when a buffalo hunter took hold of her and tried to drag her into one of the saloon's back rooms that she met Jack Kerson. He cold-cocked the buffalo hunter, and both of them ran out into the night, with two of the hunter's friends in close pursuit.

Jack soon showed signs of wanting to collect on the debt she owed him for saving her, but she made it clear that was not in the cards. She was well aware that he was a woman-izer and that he would probably drop her when he had no more use for her, but Jack turned out to be more than she had expected. Far from being angry about her rejection, he seemed to respect her for it—or perhaps he realized that she might have other attributes, that she might be of use to him. So, here she was, playing piano and providing conversation for Jack's important clients. It was clear that this was not her final ambition, but one has to eat. Clay learned that Sarah had been saving her money—Jack paid her well—and she was looking forward to an early retirement. There was an occasional wistful mention of New York, then, more fre-quently, of San Francisco.

This first night, mesmerized by the girl sitting next to him, by the pleasantness of her conversation and the warm intelligence of her personality, Clay found himself a bit con-fused. Looking into Sarah's large dark eyes, he had an immediate memory of the startling blueness of Molly's—and, of course, the warm solid feel of Molly when she'd pressed against him for that one quick kiss inside the store. He was only talking to Sarah. She was company, someone he could visit whenever he wanted to come downstairs to this little private bar. As for Molly, he hoped that perhaps she might turn into something permanent.

Chapter Five

Over the next few days, Clay's life fell into an easy routine: afternoons and evenings in the saloon playing cards with Jack Kerson, and talking to Sarah. Fortunately, Clay was, in the main, winning at cards—not a great deal, but enough to pay for his room, food, and for small gifts to Sarah. She took the money quite willingly, without pushing it away. "It all has to do with time," she'd say. When Clay looked confused, she continued, "That's all I really own . . . my time. I'm young now, and I have to use my young time to get set up for when I'm not so young any more."

That didn't bother Clay; the girl was wonderful company. She took his mind off the situation in the town, in which he was becoming involved. The tension between the Kerson brothers—who represented the town—and Henry Duval—a symbol for the county's wilder areas—was a lot more explosive than Clay had first imagined. The area's commercial interests were all centered in town—banks, warehouses, stores, mine assay offices—while out in the county there was a lot of land, which was itself, a center of contention, principally as to who actually owned the large number of cattle that roamed over the county's immense expanses. There were men who did indeed claim title to huge ranches, and to the cattle on them, but many of these ranchers were only agents for the actual legal owners, some of whom lived back East, while others were from overseas—English, Scotch, German investors.

Rustling flourished, although Clay discovered that the cattle thieves did not consider themselves rustlers. To many of them, usually cowboys down on their luck or simply men on the run from the law, all those cattle, owned by outsiders, were just walking around with big signs painted on them, "Take me."

Many of the men from the back country had legitimate complaints about the way the county's wealth was divided up. Too much of it went either back East or to the businessmen in town. There were, as usual, men who were ready to take advantage of this dissatisfaction, men like Hank Slade, who Jack Kerson characterized as an out-and-out bandit. "There are rumors that he's on the run from someplace around Nebraska, for thieving and killing, but nobody knows anything positive."

One day, Jack pointed Slade out to Clay. Several men had just ridden into town, pounding hard down the main street, a few of them yipping and skylarking. Clay had already figured them as gunmen, several were as hard-looking as any men he'd ever seen. One of them was Jeffers, looking just a little out of place in that particular company, like a carrion dog running with wolves.

Slade himself was a big, beefy man, running a little too fat—but Clay figured, from the way Slade moved, that there were slabs of muscle beneath the liquor bloat. Slade's face was flat, his eyes brutal, and his mouth a thin slash that never seemed to move, even when he spoke.

Clay saw Jeffers lean close to Slade and say something. Slade looked over to where Clay was standing with Kerson, gave a silent appraisal, then looked away. During those brief seconds, Clay had the impression that Slade had been measuring him for a shroud.

"Ugly, ain't he?" the marshal said. Clay nodded, and noticed that Kerson was studying Slade just as carefully as Slade had studied them. "I'd have had him a long time ago," Kerson said, an edge of frustration roughening his voice, "but Duval protects him. It'd be hard to get a warrant out of that lily-livered judge without Duval going along with it."

"Do you have anything worth a warrant?" Clay asked, thinking for just a moment of the warrants out on himself.

"Only suspicions. There's a lot of banditry in the back country, travelers robbed and killed, an occasional raid on an isolated mine, the kind of action that would fit in fine with that bunch of hardcases Slade has riding with him. That's what they call themselves—The Riders. Like out of some kind of story book. They soft-soap some of the locals by saying they're just standing up for the working stiff. I doubt Slade or most of that bunch with him has ever done a day's honest work in their miserable lives."

The marshal's eyes continued to track the little group of horsemen as they rode down the street and dismounted in front of a saloon—not the saloon where Kerson dealt cards, but a smaller place. Clay had looked in through its doors once and had a moment's impression of a dark, dirty cave. He'd never gone inside for a drink; he preferred the light and space of the town's other, much bigger saloon.

Kerson watched Slade and his companions until they had disappeared inside the saloon. "I'll nail Slade eventually," he said. "Some day he'll get caught doing something, something so outrageous that even the judge won't be able to paper it over. Then I'll have him, and if Duval gets in the way, I'll take him, too."

"You figure Duval's in with them?" Clay asked. "Actually takes part in what they do?"

"Yes," Kerson replied. "Well, not that he's out riding with them all the time. Not in person. He sits here in town like a spider, with his fingers working the web. He plays it careful.

Those damned brothers of his though, I doubt there's any devilment in this country they don't take part in."

"Brothers?"

"Yeah. They're not here now. They took off about a month ago—some story about going up north to see about buying a ranch. More likely looking over some bank they want to rob. I hope they get their asses shot off. This'd be a better place with them gone permanently."

Clay was surprised. There was now a different kind of edge to the marshal's voice—an edge of worry, as if Duval's brothers worried him.

The slow pace of the days continued. Another week and a half passed by, until one day Clay realized he was growing just a bit bored, and that before long he'd be more than just a little bored. It usually happened that way . . . settle down for too long, and there'd come the day when it was time to ride on, time to see what lay over the horizon. Still, here he had Sarah as safe female company—and, of course, Molly, or the possibility of Molly. He had promised the girl he'd ride out for a visit, but he hadn't gotten around to it yet, not with Sarah and the card games holding his interest. That was another factor that kept him from actually starting out for the Johnson family's mine—his present life didn't fit into the memories he had of Molly or of her mother. When he thought of Molly he thought of something, well . . . clean, innocent. Had they heard about his life in town? Would they even want to see him? He'd ride out some day and find out.

Then one day it came time to pay up on that bill he'd wondered about his first night in town—the one he owed Jack Kerson. He'd just come out of the hotel and was heading toward the main street when he became aware of an uproar from that direction. He heard the neighing of horses, excited shouting, the sounds of a crowd forming.

When he came out of the alley into the main street he saw

that the afternoon stage had come in, but had not pulled up at its usual stop down by the stage company office; it had stopped right in the middle of the main street. Only one man sat up on the box—the driver. Men were helping him down from his high perch. Blood stained his shirt and vest. From where he stood, Clay could see that a wide streak of drying blood had stained the wood below where the guard usually sat. More blood was drying below one of the passenger windows. Several people were helping a sobbing woman down out of the passenger compartment. Clay noticed that her dress was torn at the bodice, and blood stained her skirts.

Clay saw Jack Kerson and his brother, Mark, in the middle of the crowd. Jack caught sight of Clay and motioned him over. Jack broke free of the crowd, walked up to Clay, and pointed to the stage. "They got hit by five men, about ten miles out of town. They shot and killed old Charlie, the guard, when he reached for his shotgun. They shot the driver, too, and left him lying in the road. They also shot and killed one of the passengers when he tried to protect his wife; they were tearing some jewelry off her dress. That's what she keeps repeating—the way they tore at her, the way they laughed after they shot her husband."

Clay looked over to where the woman, still sobbing, was being led away by several other women.

"It was the strongbox they were really after," Jack said. "There was a big load of gold coin and paper currency being shipped to the bank. I don't know how they heard about the money . . . news about the shipment was being kept pretty quiet."

At that precise moment Sheriff Duval came into view, walking rapidly down the street from the direction of his office. "Yeah," the marshal said bitterly, "just a few people knew about the money—maybe the wrong few."

He was staring straight at Duval while he spoke. Duval was too far away to hear, but he quickly became aware of the intensity of Kerson's gaze. He swerved aside and began to speak to some of the men surrounding the shot-up stage-coach. The driver was sitting propped up against the side of the coach. The town doctor was bent over him, cutting away his shirt. Kerson walked toward them. Clay followed, and he heard the doctor saying, "I don't want to move you upstairs, Bill, until I get a better look at that wound."

The driver replied, "I managed to drive all the way into town with the bullet in me, didn't I? Gonna take more than a bullet from those polecats to kill Bill Riley. Heard 'em talkin'. They thought I was dead. Busted the strongbox loose, and rode outta there like their tails was on fire. I waited until they was outta sight, then managed to get back up onto the box. Had to leave that passenger lying dead by the road . . . more important to get his wife into town."

The driver's voice was quick, nervous. Clay figured he was fighting against showing how much he hurt.

Now Marshal Kerson knelt down beside the driver. "You get a look at 'em, Bill?" he asked.

The driver didn't seem to hear for a moment, then his head slowly turned, and he looked up at Kerson, as if surprised to see him there. "Naw," he finally said. "They was wearin' masks. Just holes cut out for their eyes. Couldn't see nothing."

Jack nodded, about to stand up. "But one of 'em," the driver said, his voice stronger now, as if fired up by anger, "the one that was laughin' after they shot that passenger fella—I heard that laugh before. It's the kind of laugh you don't forget. Heard it that time Rufe Blakely beat up that drunk miner. He was just standing over the poor old man, watchin' him bleed, laughin' and laughin'. You don't forget a laugh like that."

"You sure about that?" Kerson demanded. "You're sure it was Blakely?"

Now a new voice cut in, a high, disagreeable voice. "That's a stupid question, Kerson. How can a man be sure about a laugh, particularly after he's been shot and some woman is yellin' her head off."

"She wasn't yellin', Sheriff," the driver cut in, "just kinda cryin' real soft like. I couldn't see her, lying down like I was, playin' possum, but I could hear her. I could also hear that polecat Blakely laughin' at her like it was funny, her husband lyin' there in the road and all."

An angry growl rose from the crowd that had gathered around to listen. The driver became aware of them, realized that he was the center of attention. When he spoke again, his voice was stronger and bitter. "I know Blakely is one of them people you bow down to, Duval, but it was him sure as God made little green apples. Rufe Blakely was one of the men that hit the stage."

Another growl grew from the crowd. Clay figured that if Blakely had been here, they'd probably have strung him up on the spot. The killings had riled them up enough, and then there was the money. Many of those listening probably had accounts at the bank. It was their money that had been stolen.

Kerson turned toward Duval. "We'll get a warrant out . . ."

"Now hold on, Kerson," Duval snapped. "This is county business. If anybody goes after anybody, it'll be me—and I don't figure on going after a man just because somebody once heard him laugh."

"I heard him twice," the driver cut in, his voice still reedy, and bitter. "Heard him the time he beat up that old miner, heard him after him and his buddies killed the passenger. And old Charlie lyin' there dead on the far side of the stage." The driver's voice grew stronger, louder. "Blakely's one of them polecats calls themselves 'The Riders.' Slade's bunch. You and Slade is thicker than—"

The doctor stood up. "I got to get him upstairs, where I can get that bullet out," he said. "You gents are gonna talk him to death."

That broke the tension, and several of the men helped roll the driver onto a door someone had brought out. As the men carried the wounded driver toward the doctor's office, Clay looked around and noticed that Duval was no longer in sight.

"He skedaddled," Kerson said. "Guess things were gettin' kinda hot for him."

Clay glanced over at the marshal, surprised to see a slight smile tugging at his lips. "I said that bunch would screw up some day, do something that would rile people enough so that . . ."

Kerson looked over at Clay. "You feel up to taking a little ride?" Kerson asked. "Along with me and Mark and Luke?"

From the intensity of the expression on Kerson's face, Clay knew that his debt was finally due.

Chapter Six

It took an hour to get the local judge to issue a warrant for the arrest of Rufe Blakely and other members of the gang that had hit the stagecoach. The judge, with Sheriff Duval glowering at him, hesitated at first, but the shouting of the mob outside his office eventually convinced him it would be wise to at least go through the motions.

They rode out half an hour later, Clay and the Kerson brothers, four heavily armed men. All carried at least one rifle—Clay his usual two, the Winchester and the big Sharps, while Mark took along a short-barreled shotgun, which he carried balanced on the pommel of his saddle.

Clay was aware of a feeling of excitement among the three brothers. No, excitement was not the right word . . . it was more a feeling of anticipation, of something about to be fulfilled. They had been waiting a long time for an opportunity to leave the confines of the town and go into the enemy's terrain, the vast expanses of the county.

They rode straight to the area where the robbery had taken place. While they'd been arguing with the judge, a group of men had gone out with a wagon to pick up the bodies of the murdered passenger and old Charlie, the guard. The ground had soaked up most of the blood, but there was enough left to show where the two men had died. Naturally, the ground had been pretty badly marked by the men with the wagon, obscuring the footprints around where the stage had been stopped.

Dismounting, Clay walked around the site for a while, studying the ground. He had no trouble finding where the bandits had walked away from the stage toward their horses. Watching him, Jack called out, "I take it you know what you're doing?"

Clay didn't bother answering, except to say, "One of 'em needs a new pair of boots." Jack dismounted and stood beside Clay. "See," Clay said, pointing to a place where a man's boots had sunk into soft but smooth soil, leaving a clear imprint. The boot heels had worn down so far that the instep had left its own impression. A set of initials, a 'J' and an 'H', probably the bootmaker's initials, had been carved deeply into the leather just in front of the heel, and showed clearly. "Mean anything to any of you?" Clay asked.

The Kerson brothers shook their heads.

At first it was easy to follow the tracks the bandits had made as they rode away from the scene of the robbery. Clay took the lead; it was clear to him that none of the Kerson brothers was much of a tracker. When he was much younger, Clay had spent three years with a fur trapper. The trapper, Jacques, having grown lonely after years in the mountains, had delighted in teaching Clay the knowledge he'd gained during a lifetime of trapping and hunting. Clay had learned how to survive in the wilderness, had learned how to anticipate seasonal changes, how to predict what an animal would do, and learned to follow signs.

He had also learned how to shoot. Not just how to shoot at stationary targets, but how to think and how to react when men were out to kill him. Putting a bullet into another man before he put one into you was a matter of life and death. He'd learned how important it was to remain cool when the lead was flying, how to make every shot count. All of it had served Clay well when he'd gone after the men who'd killed Jacques for his cache of furs. Clay had tracked down the murderers, and killed them one by one. He'd done a lot of tracking since then, and too much killing. Now here he was, riding with these hard-eyed men, driven men, on the trail of other men who might have to be killed.

Clay broke free of his thoughts and called out to Jack. "These yahoos don't take much care of their footgear—neither their own, nor their horses."

"What do you mean?" Jack asked, riding over to where Clay was sitting his horse and looking down at the ground.

"Broken shoe," Clay replied. He dismounted and knelt next to some tracks. A moment later the marshal hunkered down beside him. "See there?" Clay said. "Cracked on the side. The nails are holding the shoe in place, but probably not for long."

"How long?" Jack asked eagerly, hoping the horse they were following would throw a shoe, and slow down their quarry.

"Hours . . . days," was all Clay could reply.

So they continued on, Clay leaning down from his saddle now and then, studying the tracks they were following, storing in his memory every peculiarity about them he could pick out. For the first couple of hours the tracks were easy to follow. Then the bandits, as if coming to a belated realization that someone might eventually come after them, began making attempts to cover their trail. At first the attempts were only half-hearted—riding along a stream bed for a while, then emerging further along. At times they rode over hard ground that they thought would not show tracks.

Eventually their attempts became more effective, as if someone a little wiser had taken over direction of the gang's flight. More than once Clay had to guide the Kersons in wide circles, instructing them to watch the ground carefully for any sign, and when a sign was spotted, Clay had to get down from his horse and study the sign carefully, to make certain it was the right sign. The broken horseshoe, with its distinctive shape, helped.

Finally, the bandits' tracks mixed in with the tracks of a small herd of cattle. It was necessary to follow every meandering of the herd, to make certain horse tracks didn't suddenly branch out. "Darn!" Clay exclaimed a couple of hours later, sitting his horse amidst a confused scattering of tracks.

"What's wrong?" Luke asked.

"I was wondering when they were going to do it . . . spook the herd, make them scatter into smaller groups and leave tracks all over the place."

Clay figured he could have picked up the bandits' tracks again . . . given time, and if the bandits themselves did not scatter, but night was coming on. As the darkness grew, Clay studied the ground one more time. "We should have brought a lantern," he told Jack.

"You could track them at night?" Jack asked. "By lantern light?"

"Maybe, maybe not. I sure don't like doing it. Riding along in the dark holding a lantern makes you an awful easy target for whoever you're following."

The three brothers gathered together for a conference. Clay sat his horse a little to one side, not paying much attention at first, tired from the effort of hours of concentrating all his attention on increasingly fading hoofprints. Then he heard Luke say, "I'm sure that's it. I'm sure that's where they're heading."

Clay rode closer. Jack looked up. "Luke remembered something he heard once, back in town . . . that Blakely's father has a little spread about ten miles west of here. He thinks he can find it, but not at night."

The four of them bedded down in a little hollow near a spring. At first, the Kersons wanted to stop by the banks of a stream, but Clay pointed out to them that the noise of the running water would cover sounds made by anyone creeping up on them. So Clay chose the spot by the spring, just a seep, really, but in places the water had formed little pools deep enough so that they could scoop up water for drinking or washing, and for the weary horses to drink. Clay positioned the camp at the base of a little cutbank, which would make it difficult for anyone to come at them from behind. The pools to their front would slow down anyone approaching directly.

Before they lay down on their bedrolls, Jack studied Clay for a moment by the light of the small fire they had made under the overhang of the cutbank. "Guess you've done this quite a bit."

Clay merely nodded. There was no point in telling Jack that over the last few years he'd usually been the hunted, not the hunter—often with lawmen, men like the Kersons, hard on his trail.

They were under way again while it was still growing light. At first, Luke grew confused as to the direction in which Blakely's father's spread lay, but when he mentioned that it was on the banks of a large stream Clay pointed to the northeast, where low hills came down toward a small plain. "It's the only area where water could flow very far."

They reached the ranch buildings a little after ten in the morning. It took a stretch of the imagination to call it a ranch—a collection of shacks, actually, with the house being the biggest shack. There was a pole corral, with one of the top poles missing; what looked like a tool shed; a rickety outhouse; and the beginnings of what would probably end up as a log bunkhouse. There were a number of horses in the corral and a thin plume of smoke was rising from the house's stovepipe. "They're there, all right," Jack said. "Those nags in the corral look like they've been ridden hard."

"What now?" Mark asked.

"Yeah," Luke said. "If we just ride up, they'll see us coming—not much cover on the way down."

"No help for it," Jack said. "If we ride in right now we may take them by surprise, get close enough to riddle the place. Those walls wouldn't keep out bird shot."

Clay was surprised. They weren't even sure yet who was in the house, and the marshal was making plans to rush it, go in shooting. Even if the bandits were inside, that plan didn't particularly appeal to Clay. Rushing the house wouldn't be all that easy. There were several windows from which defenders could shoot at them. They might be under fire long before they reached the house. Nevertheless, Jack was determined that they go down. "Got to take 'em before they get set," he said. His brothers nodded curtly. *They're too eager*, Clay thought. *They've waited so long for a confrontation that they're not thinking.*

"I figure we can get closer without being seen," Clay said. "See that gully down there? It runs at an angle toward the house. If we can ride along it, we can get within a hundred yards of the house, then make a break for the bunkhouse. Those logs would make good cover."

The three brothers agreed that Clay's plan made more sense than just riding down the hillside. So they swung wide around the hill until they were able to enter the gully out of sight of the house. The ride down the gully worked well enough, but as they were heading toward the back side of the bunkhouse, a rabbit bolted from a bush, spooking Luke's horse, which shied and neighed. There was an immediate shout from inside the house. "Get to cover!" Clay shouted, as he saw a rifle barrel poke out of a window. The rifle barrel spouted white smoke, but the bullet went wide. Luke had his horse back under control, and was racing it toward the bunkhouse. A moment later the three brothers and Clay were behind the cover of the logs.

They dismounted. Luke went to one end of the bunkhouse, Jack to the other. Taking off his hat, Jack poked his head around the corner. Almost immediately another shot was fired from the house. Log splinters flew as Jack pulled his head back out of the way. Jack wiped at his face; there was a smear of blood where a splinter had broken the skin.

Now there would be no element of surprise. A moment later a voice sang out from the house, "Who's out there?"

"Marshal Kerson," Jack shouted back. "We've come for you, Blakely, and for the rest of the men who were with you when you robbed that stage."

"I don't know what you're talking about," the voice called back.

Luke said in a low voice, "Sounds like Blakely, all right."

"How can you be sure, unless you hear him laugh?" Mark replied, chuckling.

"Don't think he's in a laughing mood," Luke shot back.

"You were recognized, Blakely," Jack called out.

"Couldn't of been, we was wearin' . . ." the voice shouted back, then there was the sound of another voice, indistinct, except for the word, ". . . idiot."

"You've got a choice, Blakely," Jack shouted. "You can throw down your guns and come out with your hands up, and we'll take you in alive. Or, you can go back to town lying across your saddle, dead."

"You ain't pinning this on us, Kerson," another voice called from the house. "You made the whole thing up. There wasn't no stage robbed."

"Your choice, boys," Jack called back. "If you don't toss out your guns now, we're gonna dig you out of there."

"Try it, Kerson, and it's you who's gonna end up dead," the second voice called out.

The man had a point, the Kersons were not in a good position; they were fairly safe behind the thick log walls of the bunkhouse, but they'd have to cover too much open ground to reach the house. The mutual threats might have gone on for a while, but Clay, who had glanced back toward the gully, saw a flock of quail flutter excitedly up over one of the gully's banks. A moment later he was sure he saw dust rising from the point where the birds had been spooked. He grabbed Jack's arm and pointed back toward the gully. "Someone's coming," he said, "the same way we did."

"Well," Kerson snapped, "then we'd better hit 'em before they hit us, or we'll be pinned here against the bunkhouse. Come on, boys!"

The three brothers jumped up into their saddles and pulled their horses around toward the direction of the gully. Clay had little choice except to follow. *What the heck*, he thought, *they don't even know who it is, and they're going for them.*

The Kersons reached the edge of the gully just as four men came into sight, starting up the slope. Only twenty yards separated the two groups. "By God, hold up there!" the marshal shouted. Clay saw one of the men sliding a rifle out of a saddle scabbard. He reached for his own Winchester, but Mark, who already had his shotgun on the pommel of his saddle, simply raised it and fired both barrels. The man reaching for his rifle flew over the rear of his horse, his body a bloody mess from the lower part of his face down to his belly.

"Whoa!" one of the newcomers cried out, but before he could say more, Luke shot him twice through the body with his Winchester. The two remaining men opened fire, one with a pistol, but the Kersons had the advantage—looking down from the edge of the gully, with only the upper half of their bodies showing. One more man went down, and Clay saw the fourth and last man spun half around as a bullet caught him in the right arm.

Meanwhile, the men in the house, having heard the yelling and shooting, suddenly poured out into the open, five of them. "By God!" Clay heard one of them cry, "I told you boys help'd be on the way. We've got them now!"

That might have been the case, if the group in the gully had not already been wiped out. The Kersons spun their horses around and charged the five men, who were so surprised that their opening fire was totally ineffective. The fire of the Kersons, however, was not. One of the five men went down at once, dead or hit so badly that he could no longer fight. One man knelt and fired several shots as the Kerson brothers continued their charge. Clay heard Luke curse as a bullet creased his left shoulder. Mark reloaded the shotgun and shredded the kneeling man with both barrels. The three remaining men turned and ran back in the direction of the house.

Clay had ridden wide, flanking the bunkhouse, in case any of the bandits took cover behind it. Just as he rounded the corner, Jack Kerson came into sight on the far side of the bunkhouse, riding hard toward one of the men. Clay saw that the other two men had made for the cover of the bunkhouse. One was aiming a rifle at the marshal. "Look out, Jack!" Clay shouted. At the sound of his voice, the man with the rifle spun around and began to aim at Clay, but Clay raised his own rifle and shot the man three times. The man spun around, fell, and did not move again.

Flanked with the Kersons on one side and Clay behind, the two remaining bandits had had enough. "Don't shoot! We give up!" one shouted, throwing away his rifle. Clay saw Jack raise his rifle and thought he was going to shoot the man, but Jack lowered the muzzle and called out, "Both of you varmints, I wanna see your hands in the air!"

Both men, who had also thought Jack was about to shoot them, hastily complied, thrusting their hands high above their heads. Luke and Mark rode up. "Any more of 'em out there?" Jack demanded.

"A couple of dead ones," Luke replied. "And that gent down in the gully who got hit in the arm."

"Go back for him," Jack snapped. "Bring him here."

Jack dismounted and walked up to the two men who'd surrendered. "Soames, you rotten piece of scum," he said to one of them. "I ought to have known you'd be in on this." Without warning, he hit the man in the face, knocking him down. "That's for the passenger you killed."

The man started to struggle up. Kerson kicked him in the chest, knocking him down. "And for old Charlie."

This time Soames had the sense to stay down. The marshal was clearly in a killing mood. Jack walked over to the body of the man Clay had shot. "Seems I'm always owing you, Parker," he said, "and I pay my debts."

Luke rode up, shepherding the man from the gully, who was clutching his wounded arm. "So, we got us three live ones for a hanging," he said gaily.

"Hey, wait a minute," the man with the wounded arm protested. "I didn't do nothin', so stop that talk about a hanging."

After the prisoners' hands were tied behind them, it was time to check the bodies. The man Mark had shotgunned near the bunkhouse turned out to be Blakely, but he was such a mess that it took a while to identify him. The man Clay had shot had the worn boot heel that had left its mark at the robbery site. One of the horses in the corral wore the broken shoe Clay had trailed for so long.

Jack and Clay rode over to check the bodies in the gully. Clay recognized one of them. He had been with Jeffers during the attack on Molly and her mother. "One of Duval's pals," Jack said to Clay, rolling the man over with the toe of his boot. "And Soames rides with Slade. If a man had any doubts about the tie-in . . ."

Kerson was silent for a few seconds. Then he looked directly at Clay. "I know all this bothers you. I could tell even when we were riding out here."

Clay sat for a while without moving. Finally, he said, "It was a pretty hot fight for maybes. Like maybe the men in the house were the ones we were after. And maybe the men coming up the gully weren't just some cowpunchers riding over to see what all the shooting was about."

"Yeah," the marshal replied. "We could have waited to sort out all those maybes, but I'll tell you something, Parker, around these parts, if you wait for maybes, you end up dead.

Like in the saloon that day, when Slade's boys tried to back-shoot me. Like when this yahoo here," and he pointed down to the dead man at their feet, "went after the Johnson women. Seems to me that at the time you just went ahead and acted. Shot one of them, didn't you?"

He looked back up at Clay. "It's really very simple. There's a war going on in this county, and it's got to be fought like a war." He let another moment of silence pass. "Just remember one thing, Parker. In this particular war, the other side, the Slades, the Duvals . . . they don't take prisoners."

Chapter Seven

Once they got the bandits back to town, it was difficult to tell which caused more commotion; the three prisoners or the six dead bodies lashed across saddles, heads and arms dangling off one side of the thoroughly spooked horses, and legs dangling off the other.

Feeling was still high over the viciousness of the robbery. As the prisoners were led into the town jail, several men in the growing crowd shouted out that they should be hanged on the spot. In general, the crowd cheered the Kerson brothers and Clay. After all, he'd ridden out with the Kersons, had fought the gang. Surrounded by the crowd, Luke and Mark were talking up the fight as if it had been the Battle of Gettysburg. *Darn*, Clay thought, *why don't they just let it lie?*

It was politics, and he knew it. The Kersons talked up the fact that they had been the ones to go out and tear a bloody chunk out of the bandits who had been terrorizing the area for so long. Just themselves, the Kersons, the town marshals, while the sheriff had done nothing, and was even suspected of being in cahoots with the bandit gangs.

Duval didn't take it lying down. After a conference with the prisoners, he charged the Kersons and Clay with murder. Not for the killings of the men who'd been holed up in the house, but for the men who'd ridden up—they were not directly connected to the robbery of the stagecoach; they'd all been in town when it happened. "Sure," Jack Kerson said to Clay, "they were in town, all right—which is when Duval told them to hotfoot it out to the Blakely place and back up Blakely and the others."

Nothing came of the sheriff's charge; the town was so polarized that the judge wasn't about to do anything more than charge the prisoners with robbery. There was too much evidence against the bandits, except for the man who'd been wounded in the gully. It looked like he'd eventually walk free, although the Kersons were still keeping him in the lockup. "For his own safety," Jack Kerson said, which was probably true. There was still a large group of citizens who wanted to take the prisoners out of the jail and string them up to the nearest tree.

The general divisions in the town widened, bitterness deepened—and Clay was right in the middle of it now, clearly identified with the marshal's group. To some, mostly those living in the town, this made him a hero. To many others, it made him a target of hatred. Clay was disturbed with the way things were going. The last thing he needed was public recognition. Some day, if enough attention was turned his way, someone would recognize him, someone would connect him to the events that had resulted in the wanted posters.

For a few days he put the whole thing out of his mind, searching instead for memories of Molly—of the essential cleanness of her, of the emotions she had stirred in him. So, he decided to finally keep his promise. He'd ride out to the Johnson place. When he asked Jack for directions, the marshal looked at him curiously for a moment. *Just curiosity*, Clay wondered, *or jealousy?*

He didn't try to figure it out. One morning he rode out of town, following Jack's directions. As usual, he was alert as he rode, realizing that out here in the countryside he was not a popular man.

The Johnsons' place was a dozen miles from town. Clay stopped on a little knoll three hundred yards away and looked down at it. It was half-house, half-mine. The house was large, but not much to look at—two stories high, leaning slightly to one side and the mine was right next to the house. All Clay could see of the mine was a dark rectangular opening in the side of the hill that overlooked the house. Mine tailings and other debris were strewn over a large area. It was not the prettiest sight Clay had ever seen.

There were no signs of life. Had everyone gone into town? Clay rode slowly down the hill. He was about fifty yards from the house when a pair of upstairs shutters flew open. In the dark window he was aware of movement. Part of that movement was the barrel of a rifle, pointed in his general direction. "Hold up there!" a man's voice called out. "State your business, Mister."

Clay stopped his horse. He was wondering what was going on, when another pair of shutters opened. A woman poked her head out halfway into the open. It appeared to be Jessica. "You just hold your horses, Tom," she said, twisting her head over toward the other window. "It's Mr. Parker, the man who helped us out against Jeffers and his bunch."

"Well, I'll be darned." The rifle barrel withdrew part way back into the window and a man's head appeared. "Light down, stranger. Come on in."

Clay rode toward the door of the house. There was a hitching rack a dozen feet from the doorway. He was tying the reins of this horse to the rack when the door flew open. "Clay!"

Molly was standing in the doorway, looking at Clay as if she could not quite believe her eyes. The man's voice floated down from above. "Well, invite him in, girl."

Molly moved out of the doorway and stood to one side.

The man's voice came from above again: "Might as well bring in those rifles."

Clay slid both rifles from their saddle scabbards and carried them toward the door. Molly stood a little wider of the doorway. As he passed by her he was aware of the faint odor of her body—a clean, young smell.

Feet were clumping down stairs. As Clay walked inside, a tall, rangy man came bursting into a small, cramped room. He was still carrying the rifle that had been pointed at Clay. The man's hand was out. "Johnson," he said. "Tom Johnson."

Now Molly spoke. "This is Clay Parker, Daddy."

"Sure glad to meet you," Tom said as he shook Clay's hand. "Gotta thank you for what you did for my family."

Clay grunted something noncommittal. Jessica was standing halfway up the steps. "Well, what's the matter with you two?" she asked Tom and Molly. "Invite Mr. Parker upstairs."

A moment later they were all tramping up the stairs. Tom slid a heavy crossbar into place across the outer door. The stairs led right up into the middle of a room, which was considerably larger than the one below. There were several pieces of furniture, most of which looked hand-made. Nothing looked very comfortable, but rather, temporary, although the heel-scuffed floor indicated that the place had been occupied for quite some time.

Once they were all upstairs, Tom went to the window and looked out. Seemingly satisfied, he propped the rifle in the corner right next to the window. "Good idea to keep a lookout," he said.

Clay could see that Jessica was a little embarrassed. "After the trouble with Jeffers, we have to be careful, I suppose." There was obvious regret in her voice.

So far, Clay had been watching Tom and Jessica. Now he turned toward Molly, who was standing a few feet away. Their eyes met. She flushed slightly, then looked away.

Jessica took over. "Would you care for a cup of coffee, Mr. Parker?"

When Clay nodded the awkwardness faded as the women both left the room, heading back down the stairs. A moment later Clay could hear the crash of a stove door being opened and closed, followed by the sound of crockery. Tom had gone back to the window for another look outside. He turned and saw Clay looking at him. "Jessica told me all about what happened out there on the trail. "I wish I'd been there when you plugged Curly. He's a bad one. When a man's family isn't even safe . . ."

Clay looked around the room. "And Jimmy?"

"In the mine, mucking out some loose rock and dirt. That's the way we work it now, one of us in the mine, the other one up here, watching. I'll tell you," he said, "you made a real impression on Jimmy. He's still got that pistol you let him keep, the one he picked up at the place where Jeffers and his coyotes got the hell knocked out of 'em."

"You know," Clay said. "I'm still not really sure what that was all about. I know that Jeffers runs with the bunch around the sheriff, but I kind of wondered how you all fit into that picture."

"The mine!" Tom burst out. "They're after the mine. Duval tried to buy it from me a couple of times, but I just laughed in his face. Not because of the money he offered, even though his offer was low enough to be a joke, but because of the idea of selling out before I've made the big strike."

A voice sounded from behind them, "You and your big strike."

Jessica was standing at the head of the stairs, holding a tray containing cups and saucers. There was considerable bitterness in her voice.

Tom was aware of it, too, and was also aware that Clay noticed. When he spoke, it was directly to Clay. "Jessica doesn't believe in the mine, but there's definitely gold there.

For the past year we've been living on what I've taken out of it. Nothing much, but we have money in the bank, enough so that I can laugh at Duval's offer."

"Enough so that we could leave this place," Jessica said.

Tom started to say something to her, had second thoughts, then turned toward Clay. "You see, I know there's a lot of gold there—enough to make us rich. I know mining, know when I'm working toward a big vein. The man from the assay office came out a few months back and he thought the same thing—thought I was close to a big strike." Tom frowned. "He must have talked to Duval about it, because a few days later that oily good-for-nothing came out here and made his offer."

"Tom . . . your language," Jessica snapped. She was looking behind her at the stairs, and a moment later Molly came in, carrying a coffee pot. As the girl put the pot down onto a scarred table top, Jessica said to Tom: "At least you could sell out to somebody else, look for another buyer, ask for a better price than Duval offered."

"Sure," Tom said bitterly. "Sell out all our hopes when I'm on the verge of finding what I've been looking for all my life."

"Better than ending up dead," Jessica replied. "Duval isn't the kind of man who gives up easily."

"Besides," Tom said, this time addressing Clay, "nobody from around these parts is going to bid against Duval. He's got 'em all buffaloed. He thinks he can just walk off with my mine for a few dollars. He thinks he can scare me into selling."

He made a quick glance out the window, then he turned back to Clay. When he spoke his underlying worry was evident. "That thing with Jeffers," he said to Clay, "that wasn't the only trouble we've had. There's been a few shots pegged at the house. Somebody sabotaged the mine shaft one day, but they were too stupid to know how to do it right. They're trying to scare me, all right, but Tom Johnson doesn't scare easy. Not when I know I'm really onto something big."

Clay wondered if the strike, if it ever came, would be big enough to justify risking one's family. He'd seen enough of Duval and the people that gathered around him to consider the sheriff truly dangerous.

Now Molly cut in. "Momma . . . Daddy, can we talk about something besides the mine?"

She was pouring coffee into the cups. "Do you take sugar, Mr. Parker?" she asked.

This is getting formal, Clay thought. He remembered that one quick kiss inside the store. "Clay," he said, smiling over at Molly. "I thought we had that all settled. Just call me Clay."

The tension that had been growing was abruptly broken as Jimmy came pounding up the stairs. "Clay!" he burst out.

"See," Clay said to Molly, "it's easy."

Everyone laughed. As they sat down around the rickety table, the conversation did indeed change, with Clay, rather than the mine, now the main topic. At first Jimmy did most of the talking. "We heard all about it," he said excitedly. "How you and the Kerson brothers went out and shot up that gang that robbed the stagecoach."

For the next few minutes Clay recounted some of the details of the chase and the fight. Jimmy hung on his words. "Wish I'd been there," he said. Clay wondered if the boy would have felt the same if he'd been there to see the men die—if he'd seen the mess Mark's shotgun had made of two of the bandits.

While Jimmy was asking questions, Clay looked across the table at Molly. Her eyes were open wide; she was looking straight back at him. He found himself drowning in those huge blue orbs, and he could not help but remember the feel of her body as it had pressed against him inside the store. Perhaps Molly was remembering the same thing. She blushed again, looked away for a moment, then her eyes returned to meet his.

Clay realized that everyone had fallen silent. He was vaguely aware that Jessica had said something that required an answer. "We hear you're doing very well in town, that you've found a place to stay."

Oh, Clay thought, *she's talking about Jack's little hotel with that saloon tacked conveniently onto one side*. Was so much known about him that even out here they were aware of the way he lived? Did Jessica know about Sarah? Did everyone know? Did *Molly* know? Maybe they'd get the wrong idea, maybe they wouldn't know that Sarah was only a friend.

Molly was still looking straight at him, and he could read nothing in her eyes but . . . but what? The girl was starry-eyed.

Jessica wasn't. She was watching him intently, watching the both of them, quite aware of the way Molly and Clay were looking at one another, and her expression seemed to be demanding. *Just what is it you have in mind for my daughter? You with your life in town, your gambling, your riding around the countryside risking your life?*

Clay looked around the room, then at Jimmy, who was clearly caught up in a massive case of hero worship. He'd already proudly told Clay that he was practicing a lot with the pistol he'd picked up at the site of the trouble.

Tom was watching Clay intently also, but the unvoiced questions in his eyes appeared to be different from the ones Jessica's eyes were asking. Tom looked from his daughter to Clay, then smiled a rather complacent smile. It seemed as if Tom not only expected something from him, but knew he'd get it—just as Jack Kerson had known.

Darn, Clay thought. *What did I walk into?*

Chapter Eight

Clay had ridden out to the Johnson place for relief from the Byzantine politics of the town, but he'd ridden right into a shadow of the same thing. As usual, it all seemed to revolve around Henry Duval. Duval was butting heads with the Kerson brothers for control of the town, the county seat, just as he wanted control of Tom Johnson's mine. Was there anything the man didn't want?

So far, Clay had been lukewarm in his dislike of the sheriff. Now his dislike took on new heat. He'd known too many men like Duval. Men whose touchstone was greed—greed for money, greed for power—or for both, since they tended to be pretty much the same thing. It seemed to Clay that men with money and power were above the law. Furthermore, if a free man, realizing the hopelessness of appealing to the law, exacted his own justice, then that man had to pay the system—the system that was owned by the rich and greedy.

A few years before, Clay had taken a stand against a very powerful man, and he'd wound up on the wrong side of the law. There was a price on his head, a price that a good many hunters of men had tried to collect. Some had died trying. Others had given up. Not the wealthy men back East, though.

The industrialists, that particular breed of carrion eaters, kept the warrants alive and the wanted posters circulating.

It was the land that had, so far, kept Clay free. The West was unimaginably vast, a land into which a man could vanish. And then there were the people who populated the land, men and women who had come out West to escape the power structure that ran the East. Among them were men who had been blackballed from ever working at their trades again, because they had dared stand up to the industrialists. Or men who just wanted to breathe free, to work their own land, or hunt, or ride over the vast empty stretches of the West. To men like these, Clay was not a fugitive, a criminal to be tracked down, but a man who'd challenged the Eastern establishment.

Clay now found himself becoming embroiled in a local power struggle. The situation was confusing, the dividing line between villains and heroes blurred. True, Henry Duval, and his ally, Hank Slade, were a bad bunch. But what were the Kersons? They talked a good line about ridding the area of the criminals who infested it, but Clay realized that those same criminals had the backing of some fairly decent people in the county, who saw in them a bulwark against the men from the East who were moving in, who were driving the little man from his land. That was a mistaken loyalty, Clay believed, because from what he had seen so far, Sheriff Duval and the men around him were out to help no one but themselves.

Then there was Tom Johnson—another man driven by greed. Sure, he was a much more palatable man than Henry Duval, but still a man who was willing to risk his family's safety for the wealth he believed he could dig out of his mine. Clay had, back at the Johnson place, noticed Tom watching him carefully—watching the way he and Molly looked at one another. Clay could not help wondering if Tom Johnson figured Clay would be more likely to back him if Molly was part of the stakes. He hoped not.

If he had any brains, he'd just ride on out of the area . . . before he got completely enmeshed in the convoluted struggles between the various power groups, each one intent on its own interests to the exclusion of anyone else's. He wondered if he should get out before he himself could no longer separate self-interest from reality. Perhaps he would have made his final decision right at that moment, had not something else suddenly demanded all his attention . . . movement. He saw something move, way off to his right—movement that was not a natural part of the land. The flicker of motion he'd seen just the other side of a stretch of high ground had not come from an antelope or jack rabbit, or a blowing tumbleweed. It had been the kind of movement associated with a human being, one who was trying to observe without being observed in return.

Then there was movement to his left—or possible movement. He did not want to turn his head to look behind him. If there were men closing in on him, he didn't want to give away the fact that he was forewarned. He'd rather let them think they had the element of surprise.

Riding straight ahead, as if he believed he was completely alone, Clay reviewed the terrain that lay ahead of him. He'd ridden over the same ground just a few hours before, on his way to the Johnson place. At this particular point, he was more or less out in the open, moving across the nearly flat floor of a little valley. However, ahead lay much more broken ground. If he could make it that far without trouble . . .

He picked up his horse's pace just slightly, hoping the increase in speed would make whoever was out there fall back a little, without causing them to actually pursue him full out. Ten minutes later, he reached the far end of the little valley. The terrain had risen, had become much rougher. There, just ahead, he saw the little draw he'd remembered. The trail ran right through it. Without hurrying, he rode into the draw. There were hills to his right and to his left, higher ground. He figured that whoever was out there would hold to that high ground and try to get around in front of him, head him off. The draw was deeper than it appeared from far away. Clay was able to guide his horse between some cutbanks, so that both he and the horse were cut off from view.

Clay slipped from the saddle. Pulling out his binoculars, he moved into the cover of some thick brush at the upper end of the draw. From here he could scan most of the land around him.

Lying perfectly still, he slowly studied his back trail. Yes, now he could see them, four riders coming into the open for just a moment. He thought one of them looked like Jeffers. There were two more men off to his right, and to his left, one more that he was sure of. There were at least seven all together.

They all seemed to stop, and more movement to his right caught his attention. Two men were riding back the way they had come, back toward where Clay thought he'd seen Jeffers. Perhaps they'd become confused when he hadn't appeared out on the trail on the far side of the draw. Perhaps they thought they'd somehow lost him.

He worried their confusion wouldn't last for long. They'd close in on the last place they'd seen him, and this draw was not a place he'd like to defend against the number of men he'd counted so far. They'd be able to surround him, and eventually get men into position where they could shoot right into the draw; its far end was quite open. He'd need to hunt out a better place to make his stand, because he knew he had to find a way to ambush the men who seemed intent on ambushing him. Clay returned to his horse and stuffed the binoculars back into the saddle bags. A moment's thought, and then he was in the saddle, urging the horse into a gallop. For another hundred yards he was still at least half-hidden within the draw. He hoped that when he broke out into the open it would take the men out there a little while to figure out that he was making a run for it.

Fortunately, it worked. For the first couple of miles Clay

didn't bother looking back, but when he finally did, he saw a compact group of riders pounding along after him, but they were at least half a mile back. It had taken them even longer to get organized than he'd figured.

Clay was well-mounted, and for a while he let his horse run full out. He wanted to lengthen the distance between himself and the men following him, but he knew that his horse couldn't keep up the pace forever—certainly not the whole way back to town. For one thing, it was out of condition, had been munching oats far too long in the stable. It would tire, slow, and some of the men might be able to cut across places where the trail curved and get in front of him.

Clay, though, had no intention of trying for town. He had a different destination in mind, one much closer. There! He could see it now, a mile ahead, a place where a jumble of bluffs rose, high and sheer. The trail ran through a narrow opening in those bluffs. There was no way around without riding miles to either side.

He made one quick glance over his shoulder as he raced for the shadow of the bluffs, and found that his pursuers were still just a little more than half a mile back. Clay rode straight into the opening and pulled his horse to a sliding stop behind a pile of rocks, where it would be out of the line of fire.

He reached into his saddle bags, pulling out a heavy box of ammunition. Then, slipping his Sharps from its saddle scabbard, he ran back toward the opening into the pass. Another quick glance showed him that the men had closed the distance a little. Picking his spot, he lay down on the ground, right behind a little hummock. The hummock gave him some degree of cover without hindering his view, and also gave him a place to rest the Sharps's forestock.

He quickly estimated the distance to his pursuers. They had closed the distance to maybe six-hundred yards. More importantly, they were still bunched up. Clay picked a landmark a little closer, maybe five-hundred yards away, flipped up the rear sight, and set the crossbar at five-hundred. Then he cranked back the big hammer and waited.

The trail led right past his aiming point—some scattered rocks. Clay peered through the sights, settling one of the riders into the notch of the rear sight, with the top of the front sight square on him.

Then he lowered his aim slightly. He was after their horses. So far no one had actually attacked him—not that he figured they wouldn't—but in the uncertain politics of the area, he'd better play it safe. Whoever they were, without horses they would no longer be able to pursue him.

Clay lay perfectly still, controlling his breathing, aware of his heartbeat and exerting steady pressure on the trigger—only between breaths, only between heartbeats.

As should happen when making a long-range shot, it was a surprise to Clay when the hammer fell and the Sharps fired. There was a thunderous roar, a blow against his shoulder and a huge billow of white smoke. It wasn't until the smoke had cleared that Clay was able to see the result of his shot—a horse was lying on the ground, unmoving, and a man was getting shakily to his feet. The other riders closed around the downed man for a moment, then, as if assured he was all right, they continued on toward Clay's position, riding full out.

By now Clay had reloaded. First, the hammer on half-cock, then he flipped up the latch that opened the big rifle's breech. The huge brass cartridge case, smoke-colored now, flipped out onto the ground. Clay slipped in a new round, closed the breech, then pulled back the hammer.

The men were closer now, maybe four-hundred yards away. Clay compensated for the diminishing distance, then fired again. It was an easier shot this time. The massive bullet arced toward the target, then another horse was down, the rider catapulting over its head and hitting the ground hard. He lay there, either stunned or hurt.

Clay quickly reloaded. Three-hundred yards now. Then

the kick of the rifle, the roar, the smoke, and another horse came down.

It finally occurred to the men Clay was shooting at that if he could hit their horses at will at this range, he could just as easily hit them. By now the last man who'd gone down was on his feet. One of the riders swerved by him and pulled him up onto his horse behind the saddle. They headed straight for the bunch of rocks that had been Clay's initial aiming point, picking up another downed man along the way.

Clay chuckled. The rocks were only chest high, good cover for a man, but damned poor cover for a horse. Clay sent a shot spanging off one of the rocks. Almost immediately the men were back up in the saddle, three of the surviving horses carrying double. Clay went back for his binoculars. Studying the scrambling men, he was almost certain now that one of them was Jeffers. A couple of minutes later the whole group was pounding back along the trail. Clay knew they'd have to cover at least two miles before they found good cover.

By then, Clay would be long gone. After shoving the Sharps back into its scabbard, he mounted and set out at an easy trot.

It was late afternoon by the time Clay reached town. He rode his horse straight to the stables behind the hotel, where he told the stable boy to rub the animal down after he fed him.

Clay knew there was more than a good chance that Jeffers and the men with him would show up soon. It seemed hard to believe they'd try anything in town, but he couldn't be certain. He'd never expected them to try and bushwhack him *at all*. So, before leaving the stable, he slipped his Winchester from its saddle scabbard and took it with him out into the street.

He headed for the saloon. He figured he owed it to Jack Kerson to tell him there might be trouble—but when he got to the saloon, Jack was not there. "They rode outta town a couple of hours ago, Jack and both his brothers," the bartender told Clay. "Said they got word about something or other. Went to check it out."

Was it a coincidence? Clay wondered. *How come the Kersons had ridden out today, just when trouble was brewing? Where had they gotten the information that took them out of town?*

Whatever the reason, Clay was going to keep his eyes open. He moved out into the street. After a moment's thought, he took up position on the porch of a building, where he had a clear view of the main street in both directions. Like many of the town's porches, this one contained a couple of chairs. Seating himself in one, with his Winchester leaning against the side of the building, inches from his right hand, Clay studied his surroundings. There was an alley just to the right of the porch; two long strides would take him into its cover.

He had been seated about an hour when they came riding in, all seven of them, with Jeffers leading the pack. Somehow they'd found more horses. At first they seemed not to see Clay, or maybe they could not quite believe that he was seated right out in the open. One of the men did a double-take, then leaned over to say something to Jeffers, whose head jerked toward the porch. "There he is, boys!" Jeffers shouted. "Let's take the varmint!"

Now there was no mistaking their hostile intent. Clay felt a flash of anger. He remembered the first time he'd seen Jeffers; when Jeffers had assaulted Molly and her mother out on the trail. That day Clay had given Jeffers the benefit of the doubt, had let him live when he could just as easily have killed him.

Jeffers and his men were a little slow in getting started. Thinking that Clay was a sure kill, they milled around a moment, pulling guns, before they started riding toward him. Or maybe they hadn't yet noticed the rifle leaning against the wall next to Clay; it was half-hidden by his body.

Clay took two long strides to the edge of the porch, scooping up the Winchester along the way. There was a yell from the men, then Clay was in the mouth of the alley, most of his body protected by the angle of the wall. Two of Jeffers's men raised rifles, but not quickly enough. Clay opened fire and hit both men in the body. One fell over the back of his horse, the other managed to stay in the saddle, but was hit badly enough so that he dropped his rifle. The group of men suddenly became a milling, disorganized mess. Some opened fire, but too quickly to aim well. Several bullets smacked into the side of the building, spraying Clay with wood splinters.

Clay was already ducking back into the alley. It was a short alley, with another side alley running off at a right angle. Clay walked quickly down the main alley, then ducked into the narrower side alley, which paralleled the main street. He could hear yelling from the street and the creak of saddle leather; the men, at least some of them, must be dismounting, getting ready to come after him on foot.

In this back part of town there was quite a warren of alleys and small streets. Clay wove his way through them, making a large erratic circle that would take him back toward the center of town. At one point he miscalculated, and for a moment was out in the open. "There he goes!" he heard a voice call out from behind him. Without thinking, without looking back, Clay began to turn. A rifle and a pistol fired from behind him, but even as he was turning, Clay was also moving to one side. Several bullets passed through the spot where he'd been standing a moment before. He turned all the way around and his rifle came up to shoulder level. The range was about fifty yards.

Considering the man with the pistol to be little immediate threat, Clay concentrated his fire on the man with the rifle. Firing rapidly, he hit him three times. The man staggered backwards, until his upper body had outrun his stumbling feet, then he went down hard, the rifle flying off to the side.

The man with the pistol started to to take aim, but looked down at his companion, lying unmoving a few feet away, and then up at Clay, whose rifle barrel was tracking onto him. "No!" the man cried out. He spun around and began to run, throwing his pistol off to the side. Clay let him go.

He quickly recalculated the odds. The two men he'd hit in the main street, if not dead, were probably out of the fight. The man he'd just shot had not moved since he'd fallen. If he counted the man who'd run away, that was four down and three left, including Jeffers. Clay wondered how committed the two men with Jeffers were. He figured it was worth finding out, because he was going after Jeffers. He'd left him alive too long. If he didn't take him out now, it was only a matter of time before Jeffers would back-shoot him. So he kept working toward the main street. As he drew near, he could hear loud voices—one must be the man who'd thrown away his pistol. "I'm tellin' you, Jeffers," a voice was saying. "It ain't worth the risk. He's knockin' us over like nine pins. I'm pullin' out."

Another voice, probably Jeffers, angrily muttered something Clay could not quite make out. Then there was the sound of a horse being run hard. When Clay finally stepped out into the open, Jeffers was standing fifty or sixty yards away, with two other men. Clay recognized one of them as Sprote, one of the men who'd braced Jack Kerson in the saloon. All three men froze for an instant when they spotted Clay. One started to raise a rifle, and Clay shot him in the head. The man fell without a sound. He'd been the only one with a rifle; Jeffers and Sprote were wearing pistols. They both clawed for leather, and managed to get off a couple of shots in Clay's direction. He might have killed them both, but they suddenly ran, each one heading in a different direction. Clay aimed at Sprote for an instant, then decided that Jeffers made the better target. Jeffers, however, ducked behind the edge of a building. Clay's shot did no more than rip a chunk of wood off the building.

Sprote disappeared into an alley. Clay could hear them both running, still in different directions. Following the sound of Jeffers's boots, Clay moved along the street purposefully, heading in the direction where he figured the men had left their horses. Clay's anger grew with each step. By the time he reached the area in front of the saloon, it had built to a hard, cold force.

Several horses were tied up at the hitching rail in front of the saloon. Jeffers came out of an alley, heading straight for the horses. Clay cut him off, coming in from an angle. The moment Jeffers saw Clay, he froze. He glanced over at the horses, then back at Clay, who was now only a few yards away. "I . . . I . . ." Jeffers managed to croak.

"Make your play, Jeffers," Clay said. "It's just you and me now. No more back shooting. No more gangs."

"I . . . I ain't gonna fight . . ." Jeffers stammered.

"Yes, you are. Stand and fight, or I'll gun you down where you stand."

"But . . . you got a rifle. I only got a pistol . . ."

Wordlessly, Clay tossed his rifle to one side. "Now draw!" he said curtly.

Jeffers stood unmoving, his fingers twitching aimlessly. He had never felt such fear in his life. The two men were close enough to look one another in the eyes. Clay's eyes were turning Jeffers's bowels to water. He'd never seen such cold eyes. Up until now, Jeffers, usually backed by other men, or with Sheriff Duval close by to protect him, had considered Clay a hesitant man, just a shadow of the Kersons. Now, thinking back to the day he and the others had ambushed the Johnson women, he remembered the man who'd shot Curly. The man who'd reacted like a well-oiled killing machine. That man was standing in front of him now, and Jeffers knew that man was going to kill him.

Clay read the fear in Jeffers's eyes, and felt contempt. For a moment he hesitated—how could he kill a man who wouldn't fight? Then he became aware of a change in

Jeffers's expression. The fear vanished, and was replaced by a look of gloating triumph.

He realized that Jeffers was looking past him, over his right shoulder, his eye movements tracking something that was moving to Jeffers's left. Clay reacted immediately, spinning and ducking, while at the same time drawing his pistol. By the time he had turned all the way around, the pistol was cocked and pointed at Sprote, who had worked his way around behind him and was in the act of cocking his own pistol.

Clay fired, just once; he knew, that with Jeffers behind him, he did not have time for more than one shot. His bullet hit Sprote in the throat, just a split second before Sprote fired. The impact of the lead caused Sprote to jerk, sending his bullet to one side of Clay. Then Sprote was falling, choking on his own blood.

Clay had no time to turn all the way around. Crouching, he cocked his pistol and thrust it beneath his left arm, pulling the trigger as soon as he had brought it to bear on Jeffers, who was about to shoot him in the back.

With no time for real aiming, Clay's shot went a little wide, hitting Jeffers low on the left side, passing through the muscle above his hip. Feeling himself hit, Jeffers squeezed off a wild shot that missed Clay by more than a foot. Eyes crazy with pain, fear, and hatred, Jeffers cocked his pistol again, but by now Clay had turned completely around, so that the two men were facing one another with no more than ten feet separating them.

Clay held back the trigger with his right finger, then fanned the hammer three times with his left thumb. He held the pistol steady against the recoil, so that all three bullets slammed into Jeffers's chest, in an area no wider than the span of a man's hand. The impact threw Jeffers backward so hard that his feet left the ground. He hit flat on his back, his pistol flying to one side.

Jeffers was still alive. His left hand scrabbled desperately at the bloody mess of his chest. For several seconds he stared up at Clay, his eyes filled with a horrified, stunned expression, as if unable to believe he'd actually been shot. He died as Clay stood above him, shucking the empty shell casings out of his pistol.

Chapter Nine

"Duval must have set it up."

"Yeah." Luke agreed.

The three Kerson brothers and Clay were seated at an isolated table near the rear wall of the saloon.

"That's why he was out of town," Jack added. "He got someone to sucker us into leaving, then he left too, so that those yahoos could just ride on in here and go after Clay, with Duval clear of the scene."

"But they tried for Clay out on the trail," Mark said.

"Sure," Jack agreed, "and if they'd managed to bushwhack him out there, it would have been all the better for them. It would have been just another one of our county's unexplained killings."

So far Clay had said little. When the marshal and his two brothers had ridden into town, they'd immediately been aware that something had happened—there were still bodies being taken to the undertaker. "Damn," Luke had said later, in open admiration. "Five of the bastards."

Now they were holding, as it were, a post mortem. Clay had said little because he was not particularly pleased about having killed five men. The Kersons' exuberance galled him a bit, but he understood—the ranks of their enemies

80

had been whittled down. Clay was aware of a subtle change in the brothers' attitudes toward him, as if they figured he was wholly committed to them now. Unlike the fight against the stagecoach bandits, where Clay had clearly held a bit apart.

"They were clumsy," Clay said. "They came for me piecemeal. They let me tackle them by ones and twos."

"Clumsy," Mark agreed.

"Over confident," Luke added, "but then, Jeffers never was a real whiz in the brain department."

Clay did not reply. It was done. It was over. Five men were dead—probably men who deserved to die—but still five men.

Now Jack spoke, his voice grim. "Gibson—the one who gave us that bum tip—I'm gonna have a little talk with him. I thought I could trust him."

"Guess you can't—" Luke started to say, but a man came bursting in through the saloon's swinging doors, slamming them back against the wall, so great was the force of his entry. "Jamison," Jack said. "Now, there's a man I'd trust."

Jamison came walking hurriedly back toward their table. "Got a real burr under his saddle," Mark murmured.

"Marshal," Jamison said excitedly as he neared the table, "they're here—both of them."

"Hey, slow down, Jamie," Jack said. "Tell us who's here."

While Mark and Luke chuckled, Clay noticed that Jamison never cracked a smile; his face remained painted over with the same blend of excitement and grimness as when he'd come crashing in through the doorway. "The Duvals. Dante and Milton themselves."

Now it was the Kersons' turn to fall silent. "That's all we need," Luke said.

Noticing Clay's expression of incomprehension, Jack said, "The sheriff's younger brothers. I mentioned them to you once."

"The poets," Luke added, "That's what I call them. Their mother must have had a real thing for poetry by the time they were born. I guess she didn't see anything poetic about old Henry, her firstborn."

"Dante's the most dangerous," Jack said. "Cold as ice, never gets flustered, and he's good with any kind of gun."

"Now, as for Milton," Mark added, "he's just plain mean—crazy mean. I never saw anybody that liked killing people as much as Milton does. It gets him all excited."

The sound of boot heels grew from out on the boardwalk. The swinging doors opened again, and two men walked in. Their eyes swept the room. *Alert, both of them are very alert*, Clay thought as he studied the two men, *and totally confident, the same way a powerful predator is confident as it approaches its prey.*

The newcomers immediately noticed the four others seated at the back table, and headed in that direction. Clay noticed that all three Kerson brothers stiffened a little, their hands drifting down toward the butts of their pistols. Clay had never seen the three brothers react in quite this way to any other men, no matter how hard their reputation.

The Duvals walked right up to the table. Jamison was still standing near Jack's chair. "Beat it, Jamison," one of the newcomers said tersely.

"Watch your tongue, Dante," Jack Kerson said, his voice cold.

The man who'd spoken said nothing. He simply stared hard at Jamison, who said, just a trifle lamely, "Well, Marshal, time to be shovin' off."

As Jamison turned to walk away, Clay studied the two Duval brothers more closely. He pegged Dante as the more truly dangerous of the two. There was a contained ferocity about him, a sense of cold violence. Clay doubted the man's attention ever wavered. On the other hand, the second man—Milton, he supposed—had a wild, unsteady manner, an air of random violence that could break out at any moment. *He'd be easier to take*, Clay found himself thinking. *His attention would be more scattered. He'd waste time thinking about how much he'd enjoy killing you. That would be the time to take him.*

At first he decided that neither man looked much like his older brother, Henry—except maybe in their slimness. Dante was a little taller than Milton, just a little over medium height. The one feature both men shared fully with the sheriff was an expression that suggested a total lack of human compassion.

Dante spoke again. "Well, Kerson," he said, "seems to have been a lot of action in town today. What's the matter? Having trouble keeping the peace?"

"Not since you and your psycho brother left," Jack replied.

A flare of wild, savage anger lit up Milton's eyes. "You calling me crazy, Marshal?" he demanded. Clay decided Milton's voice was a bit like the sheriff's, high and thin, but with less control.

"Yeah," Jack replied. "You're a mad dog, Milton, and if you get up to your old tricks again, around my town, you're gonna be put down like a mad dog."

Milton's face twisted into a spasm of rage. He started to back away from the table, his right hand cocked and ready. *Damn if I don't think he's going to go for his gun*, Clay thought. His own hand was close to the butt of his .44. The Kerson brothers were like coiled springs; ready to move, to fight.

Dante intervened. He held his hand in front of his brother, as if to physically stop him. "Not now," he said to Milton.

"But the son of a . . ." Milton snarled. "He said . . ." He still held the stance of a man who was about to draw and shoot.

"I said not now!" Dante snapped, his voice like a whip. "Not here, not right at this moment."

"I . . ." Milton recoiled from the tone of his brother's voice, then visibly relaxed, his right hand falling naturally to his side. He glared at Jack. "But some day . . ." he said tightly.

"Any time you're ready," Jack said mockingly.

"Now, is that any way for a lawman to talk?" Dante replied, even more mockingly. Then he turned his attention to Clay. "I suppose this is the *hombre* who did all the shooting today."

Clay said nothing in reply. Dante was looking straight at him. Clay returned the stare. Their gazes locked. Looking into Dante's eyes reinforced Clay's estimate of the man. He was a stone-cold killer with the eyes of a hungry panther. The two men continued to stare at one another. Dante looked away first, and the act seemed to both surprise and annoy him. "We got us some accounting to do, a score to be settled," he said to Clay.

"Not that I'm aware of," Clay replied, speaking for the first time.

"Oh, but we do," Dante replied. "Jeffers may not have been much to look at, but he was my personal dog. You shot my dog, Mister."

"Try a better breed next time," Luke broke in. "It doesn't look good, Dante, with curs like Jeffers sneaking around your heels. You must be crawlin' with fleas."

Clay saw the cold steadiness of Dante's eyes break for just an instant—an instant of anger heating up their normal coldness. In a moment the control returned. Dante looked away from Luke as if he didn't exist, his gaze moving back to Clay. "We'll settle up some day," he said.

"I imagine we will," was Clay's only reply. Dante looked surprised; he'd never met a man with his own level of control. There was just a moment of doubt in his eyes which vanished as quickly as that moment of uncontrolled anger. Without another word, he spun around on his heel and headed toward the door. After a brief hesitation, and a ferocious look meant to intimidate the four seated men, Milton turned, and followed his brother. A moment later the two had vanished out into the daylight.

There was a moment's silence at the table, broken only when Mark let out a long sigh. "Well . . . don't that just stir up the pot."

"Yeah," Luke agreed, "Like a stick of dynamite in the outhouse."

Chapter Ten

The dynamite did not go off for days, but the fuse continued to sputter. Clay frequently saw Dante and Milton in the street, sometimes accompanied by the sheriff. The town was tense. Even Sarah, insulated as she was in the little bar behind the hotel, seemed to reflect the strain. One night she mentioned the younger Duval brothers to Clay. "They're like two different aspects of death," she said. "Dante is the remorseless aspect; it's going to come and get you some day, as sure as anything. It's always kind of out there, just beyond the horizon." She gave a little shudder. "But Milton, he's the kind of death that simply happens. Boom! And it's there, unexpected, out of nowhere. He's crazy. Mean crazy. Did you see that little charm thing Milton plays with all the time?" Sarah continued.

Clay nodded. He had noticed, from time to time, Milton reaching into a vest pocket, taking something out, then worrying it between his fingers.

"It's the head of the devil," Sarah said, "a little brass casting—hideous thing. Milton says it's his good luck charm—that his life is trapped inside it, that as long as he has it, he can do anything he wants, get away with anything—because then he *is* the devil." Sarah shuddered again.

Clay wondered about her actual contacts with the brothers, but didn't ask. Clay was thinking of Molly more and more. Having seen her out at the mine and having seen her where she lived, his thoughts about the girl took on a greater immediacy. He was considering another trip out to the mine, but he hesitated. He did not think that this was a good time to leave town, with all three Duval brothers present. That would be leaving the marshal and his brothers in a possible tight spot. Now that he'd met the entire Duval bunch, he was beginning to think they were definitely worth standing up to.

There was also the debt he owed. It was a debt he had not asked for, but one that had been given him nevertheless. One day, he and Jack Kerson had been sitting alone at a table in the saloon—Jack's favorite table, his office, so to speak, although there was an actual marshal's office in town, a small brick building that housed a desk and some gun racks. Jack did not seem to spend much time in the little brick building, preferring the saloon.

As he and Clay sat, nursing a couple of beers, Jack took a folded piece of paper out of his coat pocket. It appeared that Jack must have been carrying the piece of paper around for quite a while; it was tattered and greasy. Jack held the paper out to Clay who made no move to take it. He knew by heart the words he would find printed on it: WANTED—CLAY PARKER. $1,000 REWARD. DEAD OR ALIVE.

Jack put the wanted notice down on the table top, still folded. "A bunch of these came in a couple of months ago. They're for distribution to law enforcement authorities."

Clay looked Jack in the eyes, and Jack looked straight back at him. "One day, it got kinda cold," he finally said, and I "didn't have much kindling. So I started a fire in the office stove with the rest of the posters. I figured you might want to have this one, to start your own fire."

Clay still said nothing, and made no move to pick up the wanted notice. It was Jack who broke the silence. "I know a little about your story—heard it a few years ago from an old coot who used to be a stockman, figured even back then that the charges against you were garbage, and once I got to know you I was *certain* they were garbage."

Jack finally picked up the poster and shoved it back into his coat pocket. He picked up his beer and drank. Clay waited a moment, then did the same. Neither man spoke, and Jack never mentioned the wanted notice again.

So, Clay was the one who now owed a debt. He stayed in town. The fuse sputtered for a few more days, then finally reached the dynamite.

The explosion occurred in a saloon at the opposite end of the street from which Jack Kerson held court. It was a gloomy, dirty place. Slade was inside, along with four of the men who rode with him and with Milton Duval.

They had been drinking and talking. Most of their conversation had to do with the Kerson Brothers, their enemies, and with the Kersons' new ally, Clay Parker, "They been hurtin' us bad," Slade said, "been shootin' the hell out of us. They killed a lot of good men."

"Parker . . ." Milton said, his voice fading away.

"Yeah, it was bad enough when there was just them damned Kersons. Now, with Parker backin' 'em up . . . that man is plain poison. The way he did in Jeffers and four of the boys . . ."

"Ah," Milton said disgustedly, "Jeffers was a clown."

"Still," Slade put in, "seven against one's pretty heavy odds."

The note of grudging respect in Slade's voice irritated Milton. He'd conceived an instant hatred for Clay Parker. Partly because, when he'd first met him, in the saloon when he and Dante braced the Kersons, Milton had looked for a moment into Clay's eyes. Milton was accustomed to having other men looking away nervously when their eyes met, but not Parker. It had been Milton who'd looked away first. He'd seen an intensity in the other man's eyes that had made him feel . . . what? Certainly not fear, the encounter had been too short for that. Perhaps what he had felt had been simply a moment of uncertainty, a feeling with which Milton was not at all comfortable. Just remembering Parker renewed a little of that feeling of uncertainty and hatred. It fostered inside Milton a desire to kill, which was the method he usually employed to settle any uncertainties. Even as he thought about it, about facing Clay, Milton felt a sharp tug of that same uncertainty. It was a feeling that bordered just slightly on fear.

Clay fortunately was not present to serve as a target for Milton's urge. A cowboy, an easier target, came stumbling in through the saloon's sagging bat-wing doors. The man staggered for balance a moment, then bellied up to the bar.

"Drunk as a hoot-owl, and twice as ornery," Slade said to Milton, grinning.

The newcomer was wearing a Remington .44 in a low slung holster. He was a rangy man, trail-hardened, with a lean, stubbled face. As Slade had said, the man was thoroughly drunk.

"One of yours?" Milton asked.

"Never seen him before."

The man's name was Harrison. He was a cowhand working for one of the big spreads on the far side of the county, a huge chunk of land owned by a Scotch land company. Harrison was a fair cowhand, a hard worker, but he had a serious weakness—he liked his booze, and when he drank, he tended to think he was a real hardcase. Perhaps if he'd been a little less drunk, things might have turned out differently. He might have taken a better look at the men inside the bar and realized he was way out of his league, as far as hardcases went.

As it was, he slouched against the bar, and bellowed, "Barkeep! What the hell does a man have to do to get a drink around here? Bring me a bottle of whiskey."

The bartender, who'd seen enough drunks to last him a lifetime, coolly produced a bottle of whiskey and set it down just to Harrison's left. A glass thudded down onto the bar directly in front of Harrison.

Harrison fumbled with the glass a moment, knocking it over at first, then chasing it around the bar top with whiskey-numbed fingers. By the time he'd gotten the glass placed upright, Milton had moved to the bar right alongside him, slightly to his left, and when Harrison groped for the bottle, he found that it was not there. Milton had picked it up, and was pouring a generous slug from the bottle into his own glass. "Hey! What do you think you're doin', mister?" Harrison snarled.

Milton said nothing. Instead, he took a sip from his glass. The bottle was now much closer to him than to Harrison. "Stay away from that bottle, you sneakin' thief," Harrison said, anger roughening his voice.

"What's that you called me?" Milton asked, his voice soft.

"You heard me," Harrison replied. He glared at Milton, looking him up and down. He did not seem impressed by what he saw. Then he noticed Milton's left hand moving around inside a vest pocket. "What you doin'?" he asked. "Playin' with yourself? You some kinda . . . ?"

Milton's expression, which up until now had been pleasant, almost amused, suddenly turned cold. Harrison recoiled a little. He was vaguely aware of a flash of color as the man standing next to him took a little piece of brass out of his vest pocket, worried it with his fingers for a moment, then slipped it back into the pocket.

Harrison reached for his bottle, but Milton picked it up again, holding it just out of reach. "Gimme the bottle!" Harrison half-shouted, reaching out again, but still failing to get his fingers around it. He was growing thoroughly confused. At first, he had not considered the slender man standing next to him much of a threat. Now he was beginning to wonder. Even through his drunken haze, he was aware of something in this stranger's eyes, a glint of uncontrolled violence, that made him wish he was somewhere else. If he could just get the bottle back, erase the humiliation—he was aware of chuckles and guffaws coming from other men inside the saloon, and if there was one thing Harrison couldn't let pass, it was being publicly humiliated. Still, considering that little hint of homicidal craziness in this stranger's eyes, Harrison might have let it all pass, might have staggered out into the street and found another bar; after all, he had not yet paid for the bottle.

Then Milton reached out with his right hand and picked up Harrison's glass. "Here," he said. "Let me pour you a drink."

Well, Harrison thought, *it's gonna turn out all right.* The stranger had tried to fun him, but had taken a good look and decided he'd bitten off more than he could chew. There was a smug look on Harrison's face as Milton poured a sizable shot into Harrison's glass. Harrison's reached out for the glass, but Milton withdrew it for a moment . . .

Then, after clearing his throat noisily, Milton spit into the glass, then laid it down onto the bar within easy reach of Harrison's left hand. A look of stunned shock played over Harrison's face which was quickly replaced by rage. "You rotten snake!" he shouted. Stepping away from the bar, Harrison turned to face Milton, while his right hand dropped down toward the butt of his .44.

Milton hardly seemed to be paying attention. His posture remained relaxed as he set the bottle down on the bar. Perhaps it was the half-smile barely tugging at Milton's lips—a smile so condescending, so superior—that pushed Harrison over the edge. He groped for his pistol, jerking it clumsily out of its holster, his thumb fumbling with the hammer.

Without rushing, with smooth grace, Milton drew his own pistol, thumbing back the hammer even as he was shoving the barrel against the left side of Harrison's belly. Milton's pistol fired, the sound of the shot slightly muffled because the muzzle was sunk an inch into Harrison's flesh. Harrison jackknifed as the bullet tore through him and out his back, burying itself in the saloon wall next to the rear door. Harrison still had not managed to cock his pistol. The .44 now hung heavily in his hand. He and Milton were very close. He looked up, his eyes meeting Milton's, his expression full of shock, of disbelief. "You . . . you . . ." he managed to say, his voice a hoarse croak.

Milton's face remained calm, almost amused. Harrison seemed about to say something else, but Milton cocked his pistol again and sent another bullet into Harrison's body. This time Harrison, his balance long since gone, staggered backwards. He dropped his pistol, his right hand scrabbling at the slippery wet surface of the bar as he struggled to stay on his feet. It was hopeless. The second bullet had torn a chunk out of his heart. Without another sound he fell heavily onto the dirty floor.

For a second there was complete silence inside the saloon, finally broken when Slade murmured, "Well I'll be damned."

There was the sound of boot heels pounding on the boardwalk outside the saloon. Jack and Luke Kerson, alerted by the sound of the shots, had come running from the other saloon. Now they moved in through the swinging doors. Jack had his right hand on the butt of his pistol. Luke was carrying his shotgun, with his thumb resting on one of the big hammers.

Jack's eyes scanned the room. His gaze settled on Slade and his four hardcases, moved to the body lying on the floor, then to his left, where Milton was leaning casually against the bar, his pistol once again in its holster. "What happened here?" Jack demanded.

Milton said nothing, simply picked up his glass and sipped from it. It was Slade who finally answered. He pointed to the body. "Fella there, he drew on Milton, tried to shoot him. Milton beat him to the draw."

Slade looked around the room for a moment. "Ain't that right, boys?"

A murmur of assent from his four men. Jack shot a sharp glance toward the bartender, who hesitated a moment, then nodded.

"Self defense, Marshal. Self defense," Slade said loudly. He grinned at Jack. "Like when your bucko, Parker, shot up Jeffers and his boys. Ain't that what you called it then? Self defense?"

Jack did not bother to reply. He motioned toward Luke. Both men went out the door onto the boardwalk. For a few seconds there was silence inside the saloon, then Slade and his men broke into loud guffaws, which were clearly audible to Jack and Luke as they walked down the boardwalk. "We oughta go back in there," Luke said, hefting the shotgun. "Clean 'em out once and for all."

"It's a temptation," Jack replied, but he was shaking his head. "It's not quite time yet." Seeing the look of disappointment on his brother's face, he added, "Oh, we'll clean 'em out all right, but we'll have to wait until they put themselves so clearly in the wrong that we can do it the way it should be done—legally."

"Yeah," Luke agreed reluctantly, "let 'em dig their own graves."

Jack nodded. "That's right." Then he added grimly. "I just hope they don't dig too many other graves along the way."

Chapter Eleven

When Tom cried out, Jimmy thought at first that he had hurt himself. "What is it, Pa?"

They were both at work in the mine, two dirty figures stripped to the waist, barely visible to each other in the dim glow of a couple of kerosene lamps. When there was no answer from Tom, Jimmy moved closer, and saw his father down on all fours, with his face inches from a seam of rock. "Move that light over here, boy," Tom snapped.

Jimmy picked up the lamp closest to his father, moved it right next to him. "What is it?" the boy asked again, trying to figure what his father was staring at.

Tom held the lamp-just above the seam of rock. "My God," he muttered. "My good God."

As Jimmy moved even closer, Tom suddenly bellowed. "This is it! This is it!"

Jimmy saw it, then, a bright gleam of color seaming the rock. *Pyrites*, he thought. *We hit pyrites again, fools gold.* If that was so, why was his father suddenly hacking at the rock seam with his pick, dislodging chunks, working like a crazy man? A moment later, Tom was scooting on his hands and feet along the narrow shaft, heading for the entrance hole.

Jimmy followed, slipping around the crude supports they had put into place to keep the mine from caving in.

Then they were in the open, blinking in the bright daylight. Jimmy saw his father hold up one of the chunks of rock and study it intently. He threw the rock down onto the ground. *I was right,* Jimmy thought. *More pyrites.* If that was so, why was his father starting to yell and stamp around in a little dance? "My God!" he heard his father cry out again. "We hit it! We hit it, boy! The mother lode!"

Jimmy crowded in close. His father bent down for the piece of rock, handed it to him. Now, in the daylight, Jimmy could see it clearly, the thick yellow seams running through the rock. He pressed his cracked and dirty fingernail against one of the seams. His nail dented it. Gold!

"It isn't even in flakes," his father was saying excitedly. "Look! There are seams of it. Seams of pure gold. My God, if the rest of it is this way, then we've really struck it!"

The women heard the yelling. Jessica's head popped out of the upstairs window, followed by Molly's. "What's the matter?" Jessica called out.

"The matter?" Tom bellowed. "What's the matter?" He was dancing his wild little jig again. "You two come on down here and I'll show you what's the matter."

An hour later all four of them were gathered around the kitchen table, on which Tom had spread several pieces of rock. Jessica sniffed a little, watching fresh scars form in the already battered wood.

"Don't know if I just hit an outcrop, or maybe a whole gold-bearing reef," Tom said, having calmed down a little. "Gotta get this assayed. If it looks like a reef, then we've struck it rich. We've finally made it."

"If you take it to the assay office, though, Duval will find out about it," Jessica replied.

"Don't make no never mind," Tom insisted. "This is our claim. I filed on it all nice and proper. If we've hit it like I think, then we can raise capital, get someone to bring in the right kind of machinery—because it's gonna take machinery to get the gold out of the ore, and it'll take a bigger shaft than that gopher hole we dug so far."

Jessica liked the sound of that. Maybe they could all go someplace where they could have a real house. "You wouldn't have to do the work, then?" she asked. She wanted Tom out of that dangerous, poorly shored-up hole. She also particularly wanted Jimmy out.

"Well, we might have to spend some time down in the mine at first—at least until we get enough ore above ground to impress somebody. If we get that much topside, then maybe we wouldn't even need investors. We could take out enough gold ourselves so's we could buy the equipment."

Jessica bit her lip. There it was again, that one part of her husband's temperament she didn't much care for. He always wanted it all. They'd been close to making real money several times before, but Tom's desire to control everything, keep it all for himself, had sunk various projects. All she knew was that she wanted her husband and son out of that mine shaft.

When the euphoria had died down enough so that plans could be made, it was decided that Tom would pack some of the ore samples onto their mule, then ride over to the next county, where there was another assay office. Even Tom, despite the legality of his claim, didn't want word of the strike getting out too soon. The very thought of Henry Duval made his blood run cold. This way, Duval would be less likely to find out—and when he finally did, it would be too late.

However, there was little that went on in this part of the state that Henry Duval did not hear about. Tom was hardly halfway to the next county when he was seen by another rider. Within a few hours Duval knew that Tom Johnson, leading a pack mule, was headed in the direction of the next sizable town. By the next day, he knew just where Tom had gone, knew that he had delivered ore samples to an assay office.

A day later two men rode into Liberty City, the neighboring county seat. They tied their horses at the hitching rail in front of the assay office. "Think he'll tell us?" Milton Duval asked his brother Dante.

"Maybe with a little coaxing."

"Yeah . . . a pistol barrel laid up alongside his head."

"Nope," Dante said flatly. "This isn't our town. The sheriff here, he doesn't much get along with Henry. You let me handle this. Just stand near the door and look at the man— just look."

At first the assayer flatly refused to give them the results of his assay of Tom Johnson's ore but after a few minutes of looking into Dante's icy killer's eyes and watching Milton play with his little brass devil's head, the man's tongue finally loosened. By the next day Dante and Milton were in the sheriff's office, telling their brother what they had discovered. Henry Duval snapped, "That stubborn old coot, Johnson."

"Ain't this good news?" Milton asked.

"Sure," Henry replied. "For Tom Johnson. If he'd of sold me the mine a few months ago it would be good news for me. Now, even if he does agree to sell, and I don't think he will, the price'd be too high."

"Well, ain't we even gonna try?" Milton asked.

"Oh yeah, we'll try," Henry replied grimly, "but now we'll have to do it the hard way."

A week later the Johnsons arrived in town, with Tom driving a heavy wagon loaded with most of their household goods. Jessica and Molly were seated up amidst their belongings. Jimmy had already ridden in ahead to rent a house Tom heard was available. "Can't leave the women out there," Tom explained to a friend who helped him unload the wagon. "Henry Duval came out the other day, along with those two brothers of his, and made me another offer on the mine. He made sure I understood I better sell out, or else. When I told him to go to hell, I thought Milton was gonna shoot me right then and there. They left peaceable enough, but the next day somebody shot up the house. The night after that, somebody tried to burn it down with us inside. If the dog hadn't put up such a racket . . . ah, they killed the dog. So I figured I had to get the women to a safe place."

His friend's only reply was, "Don't rightly know of any place that'd be safe from those boys."

The first afternoon the Johnsons were in town, Clay ran into Molly in front of the general store. When she told him the family had taken a house in town, he did not know how to react. Part of him was delighted; it would be easy to see the girl now. On the other hand, his life would be very visible to Molly—and most of his life here in town revolved around Sarah and the saloon where Jack Kerson dealt cards. Looking into Molly's huge blue eyes, sensing her excitement as she looked up at him, Clay found himself unable to think of anything but the nearness of the girl, the gentle scent of her. He was certain he could feel the heat of her body, although two feet of space separated them. Life was getting complicated again, until Sarah informed Clay of her decision.

Clay was seated at one of the tables in the little saloon. Sarah sat opposite him. She saw him watching her. She looked up, smiled. "I'm leaving on Wednesday," she said. The words were spoken with so little emotion that Clay nearly missed their meaning. "Leaving?" was all he could reply.

"Yes. I'm going to San Francisco. I've finally decided to stop talking about it, and just go."

"But . . ."

A little smile played over Sarah's face. "Clay, I've seen you with that girl, seen the way you look at her. Oh, how I want out of this miserable hole. It's been too darn long . . ." She told Clay that she had finally accumulated enough money for the move. "It's over there in the bank. I've been putting little bits away for quite a while. All the time I've been scared to death somebody would rob the place, but they didn't, so now I'm gone." Sarah told Clay about her plans, that she intended to buy a hat shop when she got to San Francisco. "I'll sell the fanciest, most expensive hats in California. Gloves and scarves, too. No dresses. Too much trouble with the fitting and sewing."

Clay listened as Sarah continued to describe her plans. "I'll go to the theater. I'll eat in restaurants. San Francisco has the most wonderful restaurants. I'll find someone to escort me, some upstanding man." And now her voice took on a darker tone. "After all, a respectable woman can't go out in public unescorted. I'll find someone so old that they can't . . . they won't be able to . . ."

Her face was partly turned away from Clay, but now he saw the gleam of a tear on one cheek. Sarah quickly brushed the tear away. "I'll be free, Clay. Free to make my own choices." Her voice was slightly thick when she added, "There aren't many like you, Clay. Not many that I'd choose to . . ." Sarah brushed at her cheek again, and seemed to be brushing away her uncharacteristically personal mood as well as any tears.

Now Clay spoke. "Sarah . . . maybe . . ."

"No!" Sarah said sharply. "Don't say it." Her voice became slightly mocking. "You're a fine man, Parker, but not such a wonderful catch. If I know about anything in this wicked world of ours, I know men. You've got wanderer written all over you. You'd resent any woman who got you to settle down. It'd eat away at you until it soured whatever you felt at the beginning. No, Clay, we've had the right kind of relationship—wonderful friendship. You don't know how wonderful it is to know a man who isn't always . . . what we've had is the right kind of relationship for people like us, the kind that builds memories. Which," she added, almost bitterly, "is all that either of us will have some day—memories to warm our old age." Then, more brightly, "I'll have my hat shop, and the city. San Francisco. Me in a little house up on one of the hills, looking out over that wonderful bay."

She smiled at Clay. A rather somber smile. "I hope that some day you'll have something, too, Clay. Something that makes you feel secure."

Clay said nothing. What could he say? He was what he was. Sarah had pegged him perfectly. He was a wanderer. After a while in a place an itch began to grow, a desire to head for the horizon. What was he doing, getting all worked up over a girl like Molly? She was a stayer, a settler. What could he offer a girl like her?

Sarah seemed to read his thoughts. "Like I said, you're a fine man, Parker, but I feel a little sorry for that girl." She turned to face him fully. "Don't you?" she asked softly.

Chapter Twelve

Clay watched the stagedriver help Sarah up into her seat. She was traveling with remarkably few possessions; she had confided to Clay the night before that she had already sold most of her belongings. "I'll buy everything new in San Francisco," she said, with great pleasure. "The money's the only important thing I'm taking out of this dump. Well, actually, it's already been sent to a San Francisco bank by letter of credit, or whatever bankers do with money."

Sometimes they steal it, Clay thought, remembering his own history, but he decided not to rain on Sarah's exuberance. She was on her way to a new life. "If you get to San Francisco . . ." she said before leaving for her room that evening. She'd already told him how she could be found.

Clay watched the stage pull away in a huge cloud of dust, with Sarah's hand waving languidly from a window. He thought of going over to the saloon to see what was happening, but changed his mind. There was something he needed to do first—something he didn't know if he had a right to do. It concerned Molly; since she and her family had moved into town, he had only seen her once. They had met in the street, an accidental encounter, but had ended up walking together and talking for several minutes. Most of the talk was about the mine. Or rather, about what the mine had done to the lives of her family. "The sheriff has come around to see Daddy several times," she told Clay, "once with those two brothers of his."

She gave a little shudder. "They scare me more than the sheriff. The way they stare at a woman . . . that Milton, he kept looking at me like a coyote getting ready to gobble up a rabbit. Dante is more like a mountain lion, just sitting there so still, looking at you without blinking. I heard them talking about me to Daddy once. I couldn't hear much of what they were saying, but I did hear Daddy yelling, "You leave her out of this!"

Clay had said nothing to the girl at the time, but when he left her, he was seething with rage. Duval was using the girl to threaten her father, and perhaps he'd been hinting at some harm that might befall her or her mother if Tom Johnson didn't sell him the mine.

The dust of the departed stage was still hanging in the air as Clay headed down the street toward the Sheriff's office. He stepped up onto the boardwalk, openned the door, and simply walked in. "What the—" Duval said, blinking up at Clay in surprise. "Didn't anybody ever teach you to knock?"

Clay did not reply immediately. He stood near the door, looking down at Duval, who was alone in the office, seated behind a scarred and battered desk. Duval looked back up at him, his expression blank. "You lost?" Duval said acidly. "The saloon is down the street."

Still, Clay said nothing.

Duval looked away for a moment, feigning lack of interest, but now his eyes met Clay's. He held the gaze for a moment, then faltered just a little bit. "What the hell's on your mind, Parker?" the sheriff snapped in his high, thin voice.

Clay shifted position a little, moving until he was at the side of the sheriff's desk and could see the other man's hands. Duval's eyes narrowed. He moved a little further away from the desk, as if to free himself for immediate action. Clay spoke, his voice low, but hard. "I'll tell you this just one time, Duval. The Johnson women, leave them alone. Leave them out of this plan of yours to steal Tom Johnson's mine."

"Parker," the sheriff said, his voice showing irritation mixed with just a little nervousness, "I want you out that door in three seconds."

"Because if anything happens to them," Clay continued with the same cold, quiet force, "if you touch a hair on their heads, then you're dead, Duval. I'll come for you. I'll kill you."

Duval was white around the lips with anger; his eyes were blazing. "Parker," he grated, his eyes tracking toward the door, but Clay was already heading toward it. Then, holding the door halfway open, Clay stopped and turned back to face Duval. For several long seconds their eyes met—the sheriff's eyes hot, Clay's eyes cold as ice. Duval's eyes faltered again. "It doesn't make any difference to me that you're a sheriff," Clay finally said. "I'll kill you just as dead. Hold that in mind, Sheriff."

Then Clay was gone. Duval remained sitting at his desk for a moment, his right hand clenching and unclenching, his face rigid with fury. He forced his hand out flat on the desktop. For a moment he was afraid that the hand would tremble, but with an effort of will he began to calm himself, so that by the time the door opened again, he was under icy control. Dante and Milton came into the room, Milton barging in, Dante moving with his usual smooth purpose. "What the hell," Milton blurted. "We seen Parker come out the door. We came over to see that everything was. . . ."

"I'll let you know when I'm too old to take care of myself," Duval snapped. Milton looked abashed, but Dante looked interested; it was clear something had upset his older brother. By now the sheriff had himself under full control. His gaze met Dante's.

"You look like the cat that ate the canary," Dante said.

"Yeah?" the sheriff replied. "Well, maybe I'm just thinking about how the canary's gonna taste. This Parker bird—we've been worried about him, but now I think we have a handle on the bugger."

Dante's only reply was a raising of one eyebrow, an unspoken question. The sheriff took his time answering. "The girl," he finally said. "Johnson's daughter, Molly—Parker warned me off her. He warned me off her mother, too. He's vulnerable there, got something going for the girl, and now that the piano player girl is gone . . ."

"God," Milton burst out, "wasn't that Sarah somethin'? I hated thinkin' of her with Parker. That's enough to kill him for right there."

The sheriff let Milton rattle on, then he looked up at Dante. Once again, he merely raised an eyebrow—and, once again, the sheriff responded to the silent prompt. "Funny that Parker didn't have anything to say about the girl's daddy—not a word about Tom Johnson. He's just sweet on the girl, afraid something might happen to her. That's our handle."

Dante was still a little puzzled. "How's that?" he asked.

"Well," the sheriff replied, "Johnson's our real problem. He's been too damned stubborn to sell out, but if he's not around any more, if the mine goes to his wife and kids . . ."

"Yeah," Dante replied softly. "Easy pickins."

The two brothers rode silently, side by side, over an empty landscape. Milton broke the silence. "I think Henry's takin' things too seriously."

When Dante didn't reply immediately, Milton looked over at him and prodded. "Don't you?"

Dante shrugged, but he knew Milton wouldn't be put off. He was a talker, and when Milton wanted to talk, he just talked. "Maybe," Dante finally said, "but he's always been a serious type of man."

"Well," Milton replied, "I just can't get used to thinkin' of Henry as a sheriff, a lawman. He spent most of his life just one jump ahead of the law. Wonder how he managed this sheriff thing."

"Maybe 'cause he takes things so serious," Dante said. "He's on a roll, and he's gonna end up a rich man, gonna make us all rich."

"You mean, like this mine thing?"

Dante said nothing and, for a few minutes, Milton was quiet. Dante knew that his younger brother was trying to puzzle something out, and since he wasn't much of a thinker, that could take a while. He was fully aware that Milton wasn't all that bright—face it, he was kinda dim—hadn't been very bright since he was a kid, and their father had belted him over the head with an ax handle.

The old man had been like that; mean, until the day their bigger brother Henry had stuck a knife in his heart. Dante would always remember that day. The old man had been about to take an ax handle to Dante, then he'd been lying there, blood all over his chest, staring open-eyed up at nothing. Henry stood over him, panting. From that day forth, there was nothing Dante wouldn't do for his big brother.

When he finally answered Milton, there was doubt in his voice. "I don't much care for this mine thing," he said. "It's too out in the open. We gotta take it over right in front of everybody. I like the thing with Slade better. Ride and rob, and if anybody sees you, get rid of them."

"Yeah, I like that," Milton said, "but we ain't rode out for a while. Henry said to lay off that until we get the mine and some of those other things he's after. Henry's got big plans."

Dante was silent for another few minutes, then said, "When you get too big, you fall harder. We should skin what we want from this place, then ride on to the next easy pickins."

"Then Henry wouldn't be a sheriff no more, would he?"

"Nope," Dante replied, "An' I think old Henry, he really

likes wearin' that badge, orderin' people around. It's like it says in the good book, 'Pride cometh before the fall.' "

"So, you think Henry's gonna fall?"

"Not if I can help it, but with those Kersons sewing up the town, and that yahoo, Parker backing their play, Henry's got a lot of trouble circling around his head."

At the mention of Clay's name, Milton bridled. "That Parker, he don't bother me none. If you an' Henry didn't keep stoppin' me, I'd settle his hash in no time."

Dante said nothing. There was no point in getting his little brother all riled up, and any suggestion that there was somebody he couldn't handle was always enough to send Milton spinning out of control, like a top wobbling along on an uneven surface. Dante didn't believe Milton could handle Parker. While Parker's usual demeanor appeared harmless enough, when pushed he exhibited a cool deadliness—which Dante kind of admired. He wished he could have been there to see Parker take out Jeffers and his men. He would have taken out Parker. He was sure he could do it. Dante had never met a man he couldn't kill. Still, thinking about Parker, about those icy blue eyes, made him feel a little . . . it was such an unfamiliar feeling that he had no name for it. Or, maybe didn't want to think of the word . . . fear.

He turned to face Milton. "We ain't supposed to do nothin' fancy out at the mine. Henry warned us. Just take care of Johnson. Make it look like some kinda accident. Then get on out. Remember?"

"Yeah." There was a petulant look on Milton's face. "How come everybody gives me orders?" he demanded.

Dante said nothing aloud, but thought, *because you're a mean little hardcase You like seeing people hurt and when a man kills for fun, he can make mistakes,* Dante himself never made mistakes when he was killing someone. The killing in itself meant nothing to him. It was just a means to an end. Henry had made him promise to keep Milton on a tight rein. It might have been better not to bring him, but Milton had kicked up a fuss, demanding to ride along. He was bored with the town—and with Jack Kerson sewing up the town, none of the Duvals had access to women. Killing that cowboy had calmed Milton down a little, although it had enraged Henry Duval. "I oughta arrest you, you nutcase!" he'd bellowed when he got Milton alone. "We don't need the boat rocked right now."

Dante hoped the job they were on would take the edge off Milton's boredom for a while. "There it is!" Milton sang out. The mine was in sight. "How we gonna do it?" he asked. "Wait until night?" Milton liked nighttime for killing.

"No, just ride on in," Dante replied. "There shouldn't be anybody there except Johnson. He won't be much trouble. Remember? His kid is in town, buying supplies."

Tom was, indeed, alone. At the moment Dante and Milton sighted the mine, he had just come above ground for some fresh air. Despite his wife's protests, he and Jimmy had been working the mine for a week, blasting loose chunks of the gold-bearing ore. The ore was so rich that Tom figured it would take only a couple of months to have enough to pay for some mining equipment, and to hire men to do the actual mining. Of course, now that he'd made the strike, he could have taken in partners with money, but every time his wife mentioned it, he would grow angry, shouting at her that he wasn't going to bargain away his mine.

Tom was sitting on a rock, sipping cool water from a dipper, when suddenly his dog began to bark. Tom didn't know the dog very well yet; it was an animal he'd picked up to replace the one that had been killed. Tom thought that perhaps there was some kind of wild animal nearby, but the dog continued to bark—the kind of barking that signaled the approach of people. "What is it, boy?" he asked.

Three-hundred yards away, Dante swore. "Damn! Looks like he got himself another dog."

"Don't make no difference," Milton replied. "We killed the last one, we'll kill this one too."

Dante didn't bother to mention to his brother that the dog's barking had already taken from them the element of surprise. Milton wasn't much of a strategist. He simply liked to ride straight for the kill. Dante recognized the signs in his brother; the flushed face, the excited glitter in his eyes.

Tom saw the two men riding toward the mine. He stared for a moment. A chill went through him when he realized who they were. Scooping up his rifle, he ran back to the mine entrance. It was a perfect place to defend himself—far superior to the house, which could be set on fire, or surrounded. "Hold up there!" he shouted.

The only reply was when Milton raised his rifle to his shoulder and fired. The bullet thudded into one of the timbers framing the mine's entrance. Tom raised his own rifle, fired three quick shots, not particularly aiming, and hoping the knowledge that he was ready to fight back would make the two Duval brothers get out.

Instead, they spurred their horses behind cover of the house, disappearing from view. "Milton!" Dante snapped. "Why'd you have to go ahead and shoot? If we could have got closer, we might have had a better chance—done something that would make it look like an accident, the way Henry said."

"Naw," Milton replied. "He was ready for us anyhow. Like you said, better to just ride straight on in and get it over with."

"How are we gonna do that, with him holing up in the mine?" Dante demanded. Now he was sure he should have ridden out here alone. He'd have figured a way to get close to Johnson, maybe find himself a vantage point from which to bushwack the old coot. Now they were going to have to pry him out of the mine, which might not be possible.

Tom was thinking something similar. He was safe enough in the mine, thanks to the dog. Figuring something like this might happen, Tom had laid in a small store of food and water, deeper down in the mine shaft. He could hold them off for days. His biggest fear was that Jimmy would come back from town while those two killers were still out there. He'd have to find a way to warn the boy. *Maybe Jessica was right. Maybe I should just sell out. Take the money and run. But sell to Henry Duval? I'd rather die.* He shuddered, thinking of Dante and Milton, somewhere out there, prowling around. *Yeah, I just might die.*

The dog was standing just outside the mine entrance, barking wildly in the direction of the house. Two shots rang out. The dog yelped once, then fell dead. Tom realized he should have kept the animal inside the mine entrance. Now he had nothing to warn him if the Duvals started moving closer to the mine.

Outside, both Dante and Milton had dismounted, then separated, flanking the mine entrance from two sides. Milton thought he saw movement inside. He fired, but the bullet disappeared into the dark maw of the opening. A moment later there were two bright flashes, the roar of Tom's rifle. One bullet passed so close to Milton's right arm that it tore the cloth of his shirt. He shouted, rolling to one side and taking cover behind a boulder.

"You hit?" he heard Dante call out.

"No."

"Well, work your way over to where I am," Dante shouted.

"Yeah? And get myself shot?"

"Not if you use your brains. Go around."

That made sense to Milton, but rather than go along the side, he went up, climbing the hill above the mine and crossing just above the mine entrance. He could hear scrabbling below him as Tom tried to get in a better position. *He's real close,* Milton thought, but there was no way Milton could actually fire into the mine from above.

Milton found Dante a few minutes later, sheltered behind a shack not far from the mine entrance. "What the hell you doin' here?" Milton demanded. "This ain't much cover."

"I think I found a way to end this mess," Dante replied.

He ducked into the shack, then began to drag a medium-sized box out the door. Milton started to help him. "Duck down!" Dante snapped. "I don't want him to see us over here."

Within a minute they were both out of sight of the mine entrance. Dante pulled the box deeper into cover, and started prying at the heavy wooden lid. Milton, impatient as usual, drew his revolver, and began to aim at one of the hinges. "No, you idiot!" Dante said, knocking aside the muzzle of the pistol. "Can't you read? It's dynamite!"

As a matter of fact, Milton could hardly read at all. They pried the lid free. Dante shuddered as he thought of what might have happened if Milton had fired a bullet into the box. A couple of dozen sticks of dynamite lay inside. Dante smiled. "This is just the kind of luck we needed. We can blow the mine, bury old Johnson, and make it look like an accident—like he screwed up blasting loose some ore, and brought the place down on himself. Henry'll like that."

Milton grunted. He didn't much like the idea. He'd come out here to shoot Tom Johnson, had prepared himself to watch the fear and pain blossom in Johnson's eyes as he put a bullet into him. Using dynamite wasn't going to be nearly as much fun—that is if they ever got to use the dynamite. Two separate times Dante tried to get close enough to the mine entrance to throw a stick of dynamite inside, but each time Tom's rifle fire drove him back. It was Milton who finally came up with a way to get the dynamite into the mine. "When I was up on top I could hear him moving around in there, right below me. Maybe we could chuck a couple of sticks in from above."

Dante was surprised. "Good idea, little brother." Milton beamed with pride, but it soon became clear that Milton's plan wouldn't be that easy to carry off. If they just tossed the dynamite from the hillside, which overhung the mine, the dynamite would simply land in front of the mine entrance and go off harmlessly. So, Dante ran over to the same shack where he'd found the dynamite. It took a few seconds of rummaging around, but he eventually found a coil of heavy twine. Taping two sticks of dynamite together, he attached them to a length of the twine, along with an old ax-head to give it weight.

In a few minutes Dante was up above the mine entrance. He measured out a length of twine, with the dynamite at the free end. When he felt he was ready, he signaled to Milton, who was covering the entrance. Milton opened up a heavy fire, designed to drive Tom further back into the mine. Then Dante lit the fuse, threw the dynamite out into space, and when it reached the end of the length of twine, hauled back a little, doing his best to swing the dynamite straight into the mine. A loud shout from Milton told him he'd been successful. Dante immediately backed away from the edge of the hill, just in case the whole thing caved in.

The only thing that kept Tom from being killed instantly was that he had already ducked further back into the mine to escape Milton's rifle fire. When he saw an object come in through the opening, he retreated even further. Then, as he saw sparks spitting from the fuse and recognized the object for what it was, he wished he'd stayed nearer the opening— maybe he would have had time to throw it back outside. The dynamite exploded only about twenty yards from Tom, blowing him back down the shaft, and knocking him unconscious.

"Whoopee!" Milton shouted, as he saw a huge cloud of dust and debris billow out the mine entrance. "We got Johnson!"

Maybe, Dante thought, but at the moment he was primarily concerned with getting back down the hill in one piece. Part of the ground in front of him had collapsed down into the mine, nearly sucking him into the hole. *Good, the mine caved in. Johnson is probably buried in there.*

Milton ran toward the entrance. Looking through the settling cloud of dust and into the depths of the mine. He could see that parts of the shaft had indeed caved in, but the heavy shoring timbers still held up portions of the roof. He tried to see some sign of Johnson, finally thought he could make out something way back inside. Then he heard a loud groan. "He's still alive!" he shouted up to Dante, who was sliding down the hill, slowing his descent by holding onto bushes. "Don't worry, I'll get him," Milton called out. Dante started to order his brother to stay put, but Milton had already dashed into the mine shaft, pistol in hand, heading for what looked like a pile of smoldering old rags crumpled up under some crazily leaning shoring timbers.

Tom was fighting unconsciousness. The blast had blown him back against the timbers. There was a terrible pain in his back. His clothes had been half-blown off him, he was badly burned, and debris had been driven into his body. He had no idea how badly hurt he might be. Barely able to focus his eyes, he saw a figure moving towards him. "Jimmy?" he called out weakly. Then he realized it could not be Jimmy— unless he had been unconscious a long time, and help had come.

"You're a tough old bugger," he heard a voice say, laughing. Tom realized it must be one of the Duval brothers. With part of the roof gone, a little light was streaming into the mine. Tom recognized Milton, the crazy one. Tom saw that Milton had something in his hand. It took a moment for the object to register as a pistol. "Let's see just how tough you really are," Milton said. Tom saw the muzzle of the pistol spurt flame and felt a heavy impact somewhere around the middle of his body, but didn't fully realize that Milton had just shot him. It took a few seconds for the realization to sink in. By then Milton was cocking the pistol again. Another burst of flame lit up the gloom, there was another impact, and this time an agonizing pain deep in Tom's belly. "You murdering . . ." he managed to say.

"Watch your mouth, old man," Milton said. It sounded to Tom like he was giggling. Then Tom became aware of another voice, someone outside shouting. "Milton! Get out of there! The whole damned thing could come down on you!"

Milton looked around quickly, just as a cascade of dirt fell in through the hole in the roof. "Gotta run, Pops," he said, giggling again. "I got another bullet for you. It's gonna be in the head this time."

Milton bent over and pushed the muzzle of his gun against Tom's forehead. Tom heard the sound of the pistol being cocked. He reached out, grabbed hold of Milton's vest and tried to pull him off balance. He was too late. The pistol fired, but as Tom fell back, his fingers tightened spasmodically, tearing away part of Milton's vest.

Tom never knew it. He was already dead.

Chapter Thirteen

First, they had to replace some of the shoring. There were a dozen men working inside the mine, most with mining experience. Several more men stood outside, watching— Jack and Luke Kerson, Clay Parker, Jimmy Johnson and the town doctor. The entire group had been hastily assembled after a man had ridden into town, saying there was something wrong at the Johnson mine. He'd heard shots, then blasting, then more shots. As he'd ridden closer, he'd seen two men riding away from the mine. He'd taken one look inside, just in time to see more of the ceiling come down. Then, realizing there was nothing he could do alone, he'd ridden hard for town to spread the news.

The rescue party had arrived too late in the day to accomplish much, but at dawn they began again. Now, by the middle of the morning, they had most of the ceiling shored up. "We found him!" a voice shouted from inside the drift. From the beginning, Clay and Jack had had a difficult time keeping Jimmy out of the mine. Now he ran forward, followed closely by the doctor. They found several miners bent over Tom's body. There had been little hope that he was alive; during the digging and shoring, not a sound had come from inside the mine. One of the miners was trying to keep from getting sick as he bent over Tom. "His head. . . ." he murmured.

The doctor approached the body. "Keep the boy back," he said, but it was too late. Jimmy crowded close, then shrank back as he saw what was left of his father. "Paw!" he called out once, then Clay and Jack were guiding him back out into the daylight.

"It's my fault," Jimmy kept repeating. "I shouldn't a gone into town. I shouldn't a left him here alone."

"That's enough, boy," Jack said. "Blaming yourself won't help."

They were bringing out the body now, dragging it on a piece of canvas. In the bright light, the doctor bent over the corpse again. Jack Kerson moved up beside him. "The roof must have come down on his head," Jack said.

"Nope," the doctor said, his voice angry. "More like two hundred and fifty grains of lead."

"What?" Jack demanded.

"Yep. He was shot two times in the body, and once in the head. His clothes are all torn and scorched, so he must have been caught in the blast that caved in the mine."

Jack turned away from the body, then walked over to where the man who'd made the discovery was standing. "Dead?" the man asked unnecessarily.

"Yeah. Shot to death."

"Told you I heard shootin'," the man replied.

"Tell me the whole thing again," Jack said.

Clay moved in closer. He heard the man describe what he had heard and seen. "Yeah, there was a bunch of shootin', then one hell of a blast, a lot bigger bang than a savvy miner would use inside a small mine like Tom's." He hesitated. "Then there was more shootin', just a few shots. By then I was gettin' closer. There was still dust comin' out of the mine. I saw two men ridin' away."

"And you can't say who they were?"

"I told ya already that I was too far away. I saw just two men, headin' off to the north."

Jimmy had barely heard the conversation, was only vaguely aware of the words. He had heard only enough to know that someone had come out here and killed his father, and he had not been here to help him. Jimmy went up to the body. Mercifully, someone had put a piece of cloth over Tom's ruined head. Jimmy knelt down beside his father. He reached out, took Tom's right hand in his own, clasped it hard, and was shocked by the dead, cold feel of it. He gripped harder, as if hoping his grip would somehow return warmth, life, to that hand. He was about to let go when his finger tips felt something hard just at the edge of Tom's clenched fist. Jimmy slowly pried apart the fingers. A piece of brass fell onto the ground. "What's this?" he said, picking it up.

Luke moved up beside him and took the piece of brass. "Well, I'll be damned," he said, staring at the shiny devil's head. "Hey, Jack, come on over here. We found Milton Duval's good luck charm."

Jack and Clay came over immediately. Jack turned the devil's head over in his hand, listening as Jimmy told him about finding it clenched in his father's dead hand. Jack bent down and picked up Tom's hand. "There's a piece of cloth in here, too. It's all torn, and looks like it got ripped loose from somebody's vest."

"Well, that does it," Luke said. "Guess we know now who those two riders were."

"Yeah," Jack said, "or at least one of them was Milton Duval. Tom musta got close enough to grab hold of him, tear at his clothes."

Luke smiled. "There ain't' much chance that Dante wasn't with Milton. We got 'em now, Jack. We oughta ride into town and pick 'em up."

"Yeah," Jack replied. "But let's look around a little more

and see if we can find any evidence Dante was here, too. I want to go all out on this. I want both those buzzards dead. I want to see 'em both swing, and I don't want to give Henry Duval any excuse to save 'em from the rope."

So lanterns were taken into the mine, to the spot where Tom's body had been found. Jack and Luke spent more than half an hour poking through debris, but nothing more was found. Meanwhile, Clay had begun walking around the house and mine area. He came back to the mine entrance just as Jack and Luke came out into the light, blinking, their clothes dusty. "I found the tracks of two horses," Clay told Jack. "They rode around behind the house." Clay held up several blackened shell casings. "I found these, too, and there's a box of dynamite over near the house that's been pried open."

Jack insisted on walking the area with Clay. Together they built a scenario of the attack and death. "Anything about those boot marks that could identify the men who were here?" Jack asked Clay.

"Not unless you find the right boots to fit into the prints," Clay replied.

"Well, it's about time we did just that," Jack said. "We'll lay some canvas over these prints, then ride into town for Milton and Dante. We'll have the boots right off them."

They got ready to ride. They were still saddling up when Clay thought to ask, "Where's Jimmy? He ought to ride back with us. He should be with his mother and sister."

It took only a few minutes to discover that Jimmy was nowhere around the mine or house. When questioned, one of the men who'd found Tom's body said he'd seen Jimmy ride out more than an hour ago. "He was ridin' like a bat out of hell," the man said.

After he'd found the devil's head clenched in his father's fist, and after Luke had identified it as belonging to Milton Duval, Jimmy had still been too shocked to completely understand what Luke was saying. Then, little by little, it sank in . . . Milton Duval had murdered his father. They had been close enough to grapple together, and Milton had put a bullet in his father's head.

Once the idea had fully taken root, to the accompaniment of horrible mental images of Milton Duval pumping bullets into his father. Jimmy walked away, leaving Luke and Jack Kerson muttering over the body. He wandered around the area for a while, still too numb to let himself really think. Once they'd reached the mine he'd had to accept the idea of his father's death; with the mine caved in, and no signs of life, there had been no other possibility. Then, after the doctor had discovered the bullet wounds, he'd had to come to terms with the idea that his father had been murdered. Then, the whole tragedy was rather vague, but now it had a face— the leering face of Milton Duval. *That's the real devil's head*, Jimmy decided. As he thought of Milton, and of his customary leer, he wanted nothing more than to destroy that face.

He'd wandered over to the house. He may not have intended it, but within a few minutes he was in his room, digging through the rickety old dresser his father had knocked together out of scrap lumber. In the bottom drawer, just where he'd left it, was the revolver that Clay had taken from one of Jeffers's men, all those weeks ago, and then given to Jimmy.

Hardly knowing what he was doing, Jimmy strapped on the old belt and holster he'd bought for the pistol. The holster was a little big; the pistol slid in too far, until only the butt showed. Jimmy pulled the pistol out again, reached back inside the drawer and took out a box of ammunition. There were only a dozen rounds left; Jimmy had already shot up several boxes for practice. He pushed six of the rounds into the empty cylinder, then put the other six in his pocket.

Jimmy stayed standing for a full minute, feeling the weight of the pistol in his hand, aware of it as a tool for killing. As this awareness spread, Jimmy knew that he was going to use the pistol to kill the man who'd murdered his father. The numbness had passed, and was replaced by a gnawing stab of hatred. The thought of scum like Milton Duval still walking the earth alive was an obscenity to Jimmy as he remembered his father's shattered head. A moment later Jimmy was out of the house, heading for his horse. Since the animal had been tied out behind the house, only a couple of the miners saw him leave.

As he rode toward the distant town, Jimmy did not think about dying, about the danger of tackling an experienced killer like Milton Duval. If he thought at all about his own death, it was that he deserved it. After all the harassment out at the mine—hidden gunmen firing into the house, the killing of the dog, the attempted fire—he should never have ridden off to town, leaving his father alone. So if he died, that's the way it would be—but he was determined to take Milton Duval with him.

It was dark by the time Jimmy reached town. The streets were deserted. It occurred to Jimmy that Milton might not even be here. Perhaps, after the killing, he'd left the area.

Jimmy knew that both Milton and Dante lived in a house the sheriff owned. The boy went there, but the house was dark. Jimmy became certain that Milton Duval had made a run for it. A sense of frustration gripped him. Then he remembered seeing Milton and Dante going into a saloon one day. He headed for that saloon. Standing on the boardwalk in front, steeling himself to go in through the swinging doors, Jimmy felt a tightening in his guts. He adjusted the pistol in its holster, and felt fear wash over him. He fought the fear, let his rage and sorrow replace it. He pushed open the doors and stepped inside.

He saw three men, but Milton Duval was not one of them. The way Jimmy entered, the violence of the manner in which he pushed the doors open and stepped inside, plus the nearness of his right hand to the butt of his pistol, caused the men to spin and face him, their own hands near the butts of their pistols.

Slade was one of the men. When he saw that it was just a kid, he partially relaxed. "What you want, Younker?" he snapped.

"Milton Duval," Jimmy said, aware that his voice was way too high and thin.

"Yeah?" Slade asked, not paying much attention. "What you want with old Milton?"

"I'm gonna kill him," Jimmy said flatly, happy to hear that his voice was now under better control.

A smile creased Slade's heavy features. "Why would you wanna do that, kid?"

"He killed my father."

"That's a dangerous thing to say, kid. Makin' up a story like that."

"It's no story. He went out to the mine and killed my father. We found something of his in my father's hand."

Slade suddenly decided to take this kid a little more seriously. He was fully aware that the Duvals were trying to get hold of a mine. "We?" he asked. "Who's we?"

"A lot of people—Marshal Kerson, Clay Parker—they all know he did it. They have proof. They're gonna come looking for him, but I want him first. He killed my paw. So I'm gonna kill him."

"You can see he ain't here, kid," Slade said.

"Yeah, I can see that, but I'm gonna look for him until I find him."

Jimmy turned and started toward the doors, but as he pushed through them he turned to face Slade again. "If you see Milton Duval, tell him I'm looking for him."

Slade smiled again. "I'll do that, kid, but you better think it over, or you'll end up as dead as your old man. Milton Duval will chew you up and spit out your bones."

"I'm gonna kill him," Jimmy said as he stepped out onto the boardwalk. "Tell him that."

As the sound of Jimmy's boot heels faded off down the boardwalk, Slade turned and headed out the back door.

Walking down the alley, he cut across to the back door of the sheriff's office. "Who's there?" the sheriff called out when Slade knocked. After Slade identified himself, the door opened and he went inside. "Well, well," he aid when he saw that both Milton and Dante were with the sheriff, "the gang's all here."

"What the hell are you doing here, Slade?" the sheriff asked. "I told you to stay away from the office."

Slade flushed. He hated being told what to do. "I got a little news," he said, "seems Tom Johnson got hisself killed."

"What's that got to do with us?" the sheriff asked.

"His kid just showed up at the saloon. He said they have proof that Milton was the one who did it. The kid said something about Kerson and Parker finding something of Milton's out there, something that ties him to the killing."

Milton's hand went to his vest, and for the first time he became aware of the torn pocket. He rummaged through his other pockets, but failed to find the little brass head. "I'll be a son of a gun," he burst out. "I lost my lucky charm."

"Don't sound so lucky to me," Slade said. "It might get you hung."

Dante grabbed Milton by the shoulder and spun him around. "I told you not to go into that mine after Johnson," he said.

The sheriff burst out of his chair and stood right in front of Milton, his face white with anger. His hand flashed out, the open palm smacking against the side of Milton's face with such force that Milton's head snapped to one side. "You could screw up taking a leak," the sheriff snapped.

Milton stood facing the sheriff, his face just as white as his older brother's. "You got no call to hit me," he said. "Some day . . ."

The sheriff moved closer, until their faces were only inches apart. He stared straight into Milton's eyes. "Some day what?" he demanded.

Milton tried to meet his brother's eyes, failed and looked away. "You just shouldn't have hit me," he said weakly.

The sheriff turned away in disgust. "Taking out Johnson should have been so easy," he said. "Now we got trouble."

"A lot more than you think," Slade said, grinning. "When Johnson's boy came into the saloon, he was loaded for bear, wearin' a gun. I thought he was gonna throw down on me. He said he was gunnin' for Milton, said he was gonna kill him."

"He said that?" Milton burst out.

Seeing a chance to cause trouble, and not liking at all the way the sheriff had been treating him, Slade added, looking straight at Milton, "He called you a gutless coward."

"What!" Milton burst out. "Why, I'll shoot that little loudmouth to pieces."

"No you won't," the sheriff said. "You're gonna ride out of town with Slade and hole up for a while, until this thing blows over."

Milton looked as if he was about to argue, but a fierce glare from his brother made him think better of it. The sheriff turned to Dante. "Maybe you'd better lay low for a while, too . . . since you were in on the killing, maybe they can tie you to it."

Dante nodded. "Sure, I'll ride on over to the next county. I got a girl over there."

The sheriff nodded. "That's okay for a few days. Then join up with Slade and Milton."

Dante left the office. The sheriff turned toward Milton. "Well, what are you waitin' for? Get moving. You and Slade . . ."

Slade was growing increasingly annoyed, but he was not about to start a fight with the Duval brothers. So he shrugged and followed Milton out the door, but once out in the alley, he said, "I gotta go get my stuff. I can meet you in an hour out by those rocks west of town." He grinned. "After all, I ain't in no big hurry to light out. I ain't got no killer kid goin' through town ready to gun me down."

Milton flushed. "You say that kid called me a coward?"

Slade just shrugged, then walked away. "See you in an hour," he called back over his shoulder.

Milton remained standing for several seconds, his face working spasmodically. His face still burned from when his brother had slapped him, just as his pride burned when he thought of some punk kid going around town saying that he was a coward and he was going to gun him down.

"A man can only take so much," he muttered to himself. "Ain't nobody gonna get away with calling me a coward."

So, instead of getting ready to leave town, Milton began to prowl the streets, looking for the kid with the big mouth. Since each was looking for the other, it didn't take long for their paths to cross. Milton saw Jimmy first, saw him walking along the boardwalk, heading once again for the saloon where he'd talked to Slade. Milton was standing in the dark shadows of a doorway, so Jimmy had not yet seen him. Milton watched Jimmy go into the saloon, then immediately crossed the street. As Milton neared the doors, they were still swinging a little from Jimmy's passage. Milton glanced over the top of the doors. Jimmy was facing one of Slade's men. "Have you seen him yet?" he demanded.

Jimmy was facing into the saloon, the man he was talking to was facing the doorway, and had seen Milton looking into the room. "Yeah, kid," the man replied with amusement. "I seen him, all right."

"Well, where is he?"

The man grinned. "Right behind you, kid."

At the same moment, Jimmy was aware of the sound of the swinging doors squeaking open. A chill of fear ran through him—but as he turned and saw Milton standing just a few feet away, as he saw the customary leer on Milton's face, the fear was replaced by the same tide of rage and hatred that he had felt back at the mine.

"I heard that you been looking for me, punk," Milton said, his voice soft and silky. "Heard you been saying things about me."

"You're a murderer, Duval," Jimmy said, his voice thick with anger. "You murdered my father. You're a rotten, sneaking killer."

So far it had been a lousy night for Milton. Both his brothers had humiliated him for the killing, and now this kid was doing the same in public. He could not strike back against his brothers, but this kid was another story.

Milton could not resist toying with the boy. "I gotta say this about your old man, kid. He was a tough old goat. Soaked up a lot of lead, and kept right on trying—grunted each time I put one in him, but he didn't back off. I wonder if you got the same kind of sand, punk."

Milton's words struck Jimmy almost with the force of bullets. He grew sick as he thought of this leering killer pumping shot after shot into his father. "You mangy cur!" Jimmy cried out. "I'm going to kill you!" Jimmy clawed at the butt of his revolver. It came out of the slack old holster way too slowly—not that it would have mattered. Milton did not at first even bother to draw. He watched Jimmy thrust the pistol toward him, but just as Jimmy pulled the trigger, Milton stepped to one side. Jimmy's pistol roared, and the bullet went harmlessly over the top of the swinging doors, out into the night.

"One chance is all you get, kid," Milton said. As Jimmy pulled back the hammer for another shot, Milton finally drew his pistol. He did it in one smooth motion, showing off for Slade's two men. He fired a little too quickly, his bullet taking Jimmy in the right shoulder. The impact spun Jimmy part way around. He caught his balance against the edge of the bar.

Jimmy was still holding his pistol, but when he tried to

raise it, to aim at Milton, he discovered that he could not—his right arm was hanging limp and useless. As he turned back to face Milton, the pistol slipped from nerveless fingers and thudded onto the floor.

Milton was far from finished. The killing mood had taken hold of him again. A white heat filled his head, the nearest thing to joy Milton had ever been able to experience. He was aware, as he raised his own pistol and cocked it again, that one of Slade's men was saying, "For God's sake, he can't shoot back, Milton."

Milton did not reply. All his attention was focused on Jimmy, what he could see of him through the white killing haze. "Punk," he said. "Loud-mouthed punk."

He fired again, this bullet taking Jimmy in the chest. Jimmy went over backwards, onto the dirty floor. He knew he had to get up, knew that his pistol lay just a few feet away, but he could not even move his head. All he could see was part of the ceiling.

Then something else came into his line of vision. A face, seemingly very far away. It took a moment for Jimmy to realize that the face belonged to Milton Duval, who was looking down at him, his features distorted by anger and triumph. "Big-mouthed punk," Milton was saying.

Jimmy became aware of a smaller movement, realized that it was the muzzle of a gun pointing straight down at him. He looked past the gun, into Duval's face, then saw a thumb cranking back the gun's hammer. "Punk," he heard Duval say once again. Then Jimmy felt one more terrible blow against his chest. As his heart shattered, Jimmy felt nothing more.

Chapter Fourteen

Back at the mine, Clay began to grow nervous. He'd warned Duval to stay away from Molly and her mother, and now it looked like two of the Duval brothers had killed Tom. If Jimmy had been at the mine, would they have killed him, too? His questions brought his mind back to Jimmy. Should he be in town at all? Would Duval go for him there? Was he intent on wiping out the entire Johnson family? Clay, standing near Jack and Luke, caught sight of the old miner. "How long ago was it you saw Tom's boy leave?" he asked.

"Oh, about an hour ago," the miner replied. "He sure seemed in an awful hurry, ridin' like an Indian, that old holster bouncin' so much. I was afraid he was gonna lose the gun right outta it."

"Holster?" Clay asked. "The boy was wearing a gun?"

"Sure was."

Clay remembered, then, the pistol he'd encouraged the boy to keep. As he remembered, he grew pale. Could it be possible? Would Jimmy be foolish enough . . . ?

Five minutes later, Clay and the Kerson brothers were riding hard for town. "Luke won't let anything happen . . ." Clay had said just before they mounted.

"Luke isn't in town," Jack replied. "He rode out this morning."

Their horses were tired; they could only push them so much. It was long after dark when the three men rode into town. Clay started to head for the house the Johnsons had rented. Then he saw several men standing in front of a saloon. There were an unusual number of lanterns burning inside. Clay veered away from the Kersons and pulled his horse to a sliding stop in front of the saloon, his boots hitting the ground before the horse had completely stopped moving. As he stepped up onto the boardwalk, he saw the town doctor coming out of the saloon's swinging doors. The grim look on the doctor's face when he saw him was like a blow to Clay. "What's happened?" he asked the doctor. "Is it the boy?"

The doctor nodded. Clay pushed by him into the saloon. Several men were standing around Jimmy's body. Clay pushed them aside, forced himself to look.

The boy lay flat on his back, his eyes half open, his face twisted into a grimace of . . . fear? Pain? Clay grabbed one of the men by the shoulder. "What happened?" he demanded.

"Hey, let go of me, Mister," the man said, flinching away from the force of Clay's grip. "I just got here." Seeing the look on Clay's face, he added, "Ask the barkeep. He's the one who's been doing all the talking."

Clay turned and saw that Jack Kerson was standing with a man wearing a dirty apron. Clay walked closer. "Yeah," the man was saying to Jack, "they was all in here—Milton Duval, with Slade and three of his boys—but none of Slade's bunch had anything to do with it. It was just Milton. He shot the kid."

Then, as if remembering who his best customers were, he added, "The kid, though, he came in here looking for Milton, twice. He said he was gonna kill him, and he shot first. Old Milton, he didn't have much choice."

Luke came in, and faced with two of his brothers and with that newcomer staring so hard at him—the one who'd wiped out Jeffers and his men like they were six year old kids—the entire story quickly came out. Now the bartender began trying to ingratiate himself with the current threat. "Yeah," he said. "The kid was down on the floor, probably dying, and Duval, he just stood over him, cocked his piece, said something, and put one last bullet into him."

Jack had a few more questions to ask, but then noticed that Clay was no longer in the saloon. "Did anybody see Parker leave?" he asked.

"Yeah," one of the bystanders said. "He walked out a couple of minutes ago—stopped by his horse a minute, grabbed his Winchester, then took off up the street."

Since the house where the Duvals were staying was in the opposite direction, Jack headed for the sheriff's office. "Come on, Luke," he called back over his shoulder. "I think we got us a problem."

Jack could see light spilling out into the street from the sheriff's office; the door was wide open. He walked up to the open door. Looking inside, he saw Clay standing just inside the doorway. On the far side of the room, Henry Duval was standing with his back to the wall, facing Clay, his face white. "Parker," he was saying, "you can't . . ."

"I told you before," Clay said, not so much in reply, but as a flat statement. "I came in here and warned you to stay away from the Johnsons. You didn't, and a man and his son are dead. Now I'm going to kill you, Duval."

"Are you crazy, Parker?" the sheriff demanded, his voice strained. "Ask anybody . . . I've been in town for the past three days. I didn't have anything to do with . . ."

"You turned those two hyenas loose, Duval," Clay said, his voice devoid of all emotion. "Now go for your gun, or I'll shoot you down like the dog you are."

The sheriff tried to reply, but discovered that his voice was no longer functioning. He'd heard about the boy's death only a few minutes earlier, and had privately cursed Milton's idiocy. Now it looked as if he'd come to the end of his trail. He had no doubt that the man facing him was going to kill him. He saw his death in those icy blue eyes, in the cold set of Parker's features, the certainty of his manner. Duval knew that even if he fought back it would end the same. Parker would kill him. The sheriff felt a weakening of the muscles in his abdomen—in another few seconds he would foul himself.

Then he saw movement in the office doorway, Jack and Luke Kerson appear right behind Parker. For a moment, the sheriff knew even greater fear. They had all come here to kill him. Then he heard Jack Kerson saying, "No, Clay. This isn't the way. We got 'em cold to rights. We can do this all nice and legal. Milton and Dante are both gonna hang."

"Don't interfere, Jack," Clay said. "The first one of them's going to die right now."

All of Duval's fear returned. There would be no stopping Parker from killing him. He could still see it in the man's eyes. Then the marshal spoke again. "I know I don't have to tell you, Clay . . . there's nothing that'd make me happier than to see Henry Duval lying dead. If you kill him now, though, we may never get our chance at Milton and Dante. They'll skate away free, while the law's all wrapped up with you for gunning down a sheriff. You know how that works, don't you, Clay?"

To Duval's amazement, whatever Kerson meant, seemed to get through to Parker. The sheriff felt a lessening of the intensity of Parker's manner. Clay finally turned away from the sheriff. "All right, Jack. We'll try it your way—but if it doesn't work, I'm going after them." His attention turned back toward Duval, who flinched away. "Starting with him."

A moment later Clay had walked out the door. Seeing him gone, Duval felt his confidence returning. "You keep him on a leash, Kerson," he said to Jack, "or he's the one who's going to swing."

"Oh shut up," Jack said to the sheriff. He looked Duval straight in the eyes. "If we don't get our hands on those two mad-dog brothers of yours, Parker won't come looking for you alone. I'll be right alongside him."

Once out of the sheriff's office, Clay walked stiffly down the street, still holding his rifle. He considered taking it back to his horse, but he knew that he had something else to do first. He kept heading down the street, then turned down another street. In a few minutes he was standing in front of the Johnson house. Lamps seemed to be burning in every room. The doctor came out. "How are they?" Clay asked.

The doctor shrugged. "Different than I expected. No hysterics. You'll find a couple of strong women in there."

Clay walked past him and went to the front door. It was wide open. Clay saw Jessica standing in the center of the living room, talking to another woman. He went inside. When Jessica saw Clay, she looked straight at him. The doctor had been right. Jessica seemed to be exerting an iron-willed calm. "Did you see them?" she asked. "Did you see both Tom and Jimmy? Did you see them . . . lying there dead?"

Clay realized that Jessica's calm was only a thin, hard shell, barely able to contain her pain. He merely nodded. He didn't want to say anything about how her husband's corpse had looked, or the look of horror on her dead son's face.

"I suppose they think they're going to get the mine, now that Tom and Jimmy are dead," Jessica continued, "but they're wrong. Do they think they can simply kill my men, and then profit from their murders?"

Clay didn't know what to say. He thought it might be better to let her talk, because if she was quiet too long she would probably fall apart.

"I've been talking to Mr. Adams," Jessica said. "He told me he can find a manager to run the mine, that it's rich enough to support a manager and good-sized crew. If Tom had done that, if he hadn't been so intent on hanging onto every nickel's worth of gold . . . that was Tom's weakness. He had to control everything himself, and now he's . . . Jimmy's . . ." She squared her shoulders. "I just won't let those Duvals profit by their murders. They'd have to kill me, too."

Clay nodded. A few days ago they might have done just that, but now, with so much uproar over Tom and Jimmy's deaths, he figured the Duvals might lie low for a while. They might leave the women alone. With the mine being run by professionals, it would be out of their reach.

It would have been cleaner, more certain, to kill Henry Duval tonight, then go after his two brothers. Jack had been right. Killing a sheriff could stir up a lot of trouble, and shift attention to himself, rather than Milton and Dante.

It was strange, seeing Jack Kerson suddenly so concerned with the letter of the law. Maybe he figured he had his enemies on the run now, and didn't want to make any mistakes that might let them escape. Jack did seem to genuinely hate Henry Duval.

Clay saw movement through another doorway. It was Molly. She was standing in one of the bedrooms, looking straight at him. Her expression was remote, just a little vague, but her eyes were hot, compelling. He went to her and started to reach out, but she did not respond physically, did not come into his arms. "Are they dead?" she asked flatly.

At first he thought she was talking about her father and brother. Then he realized she meant the Duvals. "Not yet," he replied.

"Why not?" she asked, her manner not one of accusation, but rather of wonder. "Why should they be alive, and . . . ?"

"They'll hang."

She laughed, a short, derisive snort of laughter. "Do you really believe that?" she asked scornfully. "They'll slip out of this like they slip out of everything. I want to see them dead now. I want all three of them lying dead in the street. I thought you would . . ."

"The marshal stopped me from killing the sheriff." It sounded lame even as he was thinking the words.

Molly seemed amazed. "Jack did that?" she asked. She did come to him then, stood right in front of him, her blouse brushing the front of his shirt. When she looked up at him, her eyes met his with a disturbing intensity—an intensity that was cold rather than affectionate. "You'll kill them for me, Clay." The words were spoken matter of factly, while she finally pressed her body against his.

He could feel the length of her, the softness. He could sense the places where her body curved. He had thought for a moment that, like Jessica, the girl was on the verge of emotional collapse. Then he realized that she was under complete control, and all of her personal force was centered on the destruction of the three brothers who had killed her men. All of her femininity was at the service of that goal. If necessary, that femininity, her desirableness would be used on Clay, to motivate him to destroy her enemies. Looking into those large blue eyes, which he had always thought of as filled with such softness and sensuality, he now saw only a cold, hard purpose. He had to repress a shudder.

Molly moved away then, her right hand trailing over his chest as she left him. For several seconds she stood facing him, her eyes holding his. He turned away, and as he left the room to go back to Jessica, he heard Molly say one more time. "Kill them for me, Clay. Kill them for us." Then, as if she wanted to make certain he knew what she was offering, she added, "Kill them for you and me."

Chapter Fifteen

Molly was right; it looked as if the Duvals were not going to hang. The local judge was still controlled by the sheriff. He simply refused to issue a warrant. "Ain't nobody actually saw them boys kill Tom Johnson," he said stubbornly.

"But" Jack Kerson burst out, "they found Milton's good luck charm clutched in Tom's dead fist."

"Still don't mean nothing," the judge replied. "Tom coulda picked up that charm anywhere. I ain't gonna issue a warrant just 'cause you got it in for the Duvals, Marshal."

Jack could see no point in wasting any more time. As he turned to leave, he said to the judge, "I'll tell you one thing, you crooked old snake, if those boys commit any more outrages, you're gonna do a lot of hurting . . . Your Honor."

"Are you threatening me?" the judge sputtered.

Since the only other person present was Luke, Jack replied. "You bet I am, but it isn't gonna be me coming after you. It's gonna be Clay Parker. You remember Clay Parker, judge? He's real heated up about this, and real close to the Johnson family. He wants Milton and Dante very, very, badly. If there's any more trouble, and he figures it was all because of you . . ."

By then Jack and Luke were moving out the door, leaving

133

the judge to ruminate. Yes, he remembered Clay Parker, remembered how cold Parker's eyes had been that other time when he'd been expecting a warrant. The judge sighed. He'd given in that time and taken hell for it from Henry Duval— a man who, along with his brothers, he feared even more than he feared Parker. There'd be no warrants for now.

That is, if the Duval boys managed to stay out of trouble which was one hell of a big if. They were real wild boys, particularly Milton, although the judge had enough brains to realize that Dante was the deadlier of the two. The judge hoped they'd just lay low for a while . . .

Lying low did not particularly suit the two Duval brothers. After a week with Slade's bunch, both Dante and Milton found themselves intolerably bored. "How long we gotta stay in this hole?" Milton asked one day.

"Until Henry tells us we can go back," Dante replied, but without much enthusiasm.

"But what the hell for?" Milton demanded. "We know there ain't gonna be no warrants."

"Maybe, maybe not—that damned Jack Kerson took off for the circuit court. He figures he can talk them into issuing a warrant."

"So what? Henry'll make sure they never convict us, not in his town."

"I'll tell you so what: Henry's up for election in a few weeks. He says that having us wandering around town, with this Johnson thing hanging over our heads, might cost him the election. Then where would we be? The way it is now, with Henry as sheriff, we can pretty much do what we want."

"Then, like I said, why are we hanging around this dump? I wanna hit a town and do some howlin'."

"That's pretty hard to do much without any money," Dante replied, but with just a touch of bitterness. He, like Milton, was not particularly happy about the situation. Slade's place was a collection of hastily thrown-together shacks in a box canyon, way out in the middle of the badlands. It was an easy place to defend, but dirty, cold, and boring. He and Milton had made several trips to the neighboring county, frequenting the bars and brothels . . . as long as they'd had money. Now though, there was none left; neither brother was particularly thrifty with money, not where booze and women were concerned. This exile was beginning to grate on Dante almost as much as it grated on Milton. He knew one of the reasons Henry didn't want them back in town was because of the Kerson brothers and that strange *hombre*, Parker. On one of his trips to the hideout, the sheriff had told his brothers that there was no way to tell what the Kersons might do. "They might not even care about a warrant," he said. "They may just go for you."

"Let 'em," Milton had burst out. "I ain't scared of any of them."

Dante had said nothing, but he was galled at the idea of hiding from anyone . . . election or not. He also wanted some female companionship and needed some money. He sat on a rock, thinking about a girl who worked in a saloon over in the neighboring county seat. She was only sixteen, easily cowed and afraid of him. Dante loved to see the spark of fear in her eyes when he walked into the room. He cultivated that fear, hurting the girl just enough to instill terror, but not enough to ruin her. The saloon she worked in was run on no-nonsense business principles—no money, no time with the girl. "Damn!" he burst out.

Slade had been watching the two men; he was standing just a few yards away, had overheard most of what they'd said and enjoyed every word of it. He was still rankling from the way Dante and the sheriff had treated him the last time he was in town—like he was their errand boy, the high and mighty Duvals. He'd like to ship both of them out, but he wasn't ready to break with Henry Duval, not quite yet. He could use Dante and Milton, use their guns. "Hey, boys," he said, walking towards them. "How'd you like to pick up a pile of money?"

The question immediately gained him their attention. "How?" Milton blurted.

"Simple. Robbin' from the rich to give to the poor—which is us. I got word earlier today that there's a supply train runnin' out to that big mine over on the other side of the county, whole passle o' wagons."

Neither Dante nor Milton looked at all interested. "They'll be carrying mining equipment," Slade continued, "food for the miners and," he added, "the whole month's payroll—maybe twenty thousand dollars."

"Damn," Milton said.

Dante said nothing at first, but he no longer looked bored. "When . . . and where?" he finally asked.

"They should be passin' not more'n ten miles from here, some time tomorrow. I got a man watchin' 'em." Slade smiled. "You boys interested?"

There were five wagons strung out along the trail, moving slowly, the iron-rimmed wheels sinking into the soft earth. The wagons were heavily loaded, as Slade had said, mostly with mining equipment and living supplies.

It was not the supplies that weighed most heavily on the wagon boss's mind. It was the padlocked iron chests in one of the wagons, crammed with gold and silver coins and banknotes—the mine payroll.

John Simpson was not a wagon boss by trade. He was a mining foreman, but his bosses, when they heard he'd done some haulage work in the past, had dragooned him into the job. *Tight-fisted varmints*, he thought, *they wouldn't shell out the money to hire a regular wagon boss, nor would they pay for professional guards. There should be Pinkertons riding perimeter, but the Pinkerton Agency, blast their rotten souls, charge plenty—the bunch of labor-bashing scoundrels.* Simpson had a scar on his forehead made by a Pinkerton club back when Simpson had been younger and saltier, and had joined in a work protest. The Pinks had broken that up fast enough. He wished he had three or four of them along right now. The only guards he had were two miners, handed rifles and shotguns, and forced into this thing just as he'd been. Neither one of them was a natural fighter.

Simpson cursed under his breath. This was rough country, plenty of hardcases out here. He'd be glad when they sighted the mine, as much as he hated mines. He'd been working in them since he was a kid, and despite the odds, the back-breaking work, the danger, the high loss of life among his fellow miners, the lung diseases, he'd managed to survive—had even saved up a little money. He was nearly sixty, and felt it was time to head out to Oregon, buy himself a little place, stock it with a cow or two, a few chickens, and spend the rest of his life fishing.

While Simpson was daydreaming about clear mountain streams, a quarter of a mile away a man sat his horse, hidden among a stand of willows down by a stream bed. He was Slade's man, and had been keeping track of the train since it set out for the mine. It had been no trick to get ahead of the lumbering, overloaded wagons, then ride to warn Slade they were on their way. Slade and his gang were behind a hill a few hundred yards back. The man would have been with them, but there was a fork in the trail a few hundred yards ahead. It was his job to see which fork the wagons took.

To the man's relief, the wagons took the right-hand fork, which would take them past a stand of huge boulders another two miles ahead. The watcher immediately spurred his horse away from the road. In a few minutes he was with the gang. "They did like I figured," he told Slade. "They oughta be at the rocks in half an hour."

Slade grinned, then turned to his men. "Let's ride, boys. It's payday."

"Better be," Milton Duval groused. "I'm tired of sittin' on this nag."

When Simpson reached the fork in the road, he'd had to make a decision he'd been putting off. The left fork would put him on the long road to the mine. The right fork was a more direct route, but also led through rougher, broken, more isolated country. It was a good place for an ambush, but if he took the left fork, he'd be caught out in the open at night. So he decided on the right fork.

He'd been over this particular trail only once before, so when he sighted the stand of boulders he was a little surprised; he'd forgotten they were there. They lay about fifty yards off to the left of the trail, at a point where the trail narrowed, hemmed in by a low cliff on the right. He signaled one of the guards over to his wagon. "You keep a good lookout," he told the man. "There's kind of a tight spot up ahead."

The guard nodded, although he hadn't been paying much attention. He figured Simpson for a fussy old lady, worried about everything. This was the easiest job the man had had for a long time. Just ride a horse, and look around a lot, pretend he was an Indian scout. He thought maybe he'd see if he couldn't get some kind of permanent job as guard, maybe even at the mine—anything to keep from going down the hole again. Simpson had some clout at the mine, so he'd better look alive. He rode away from the wagons, heading toward the pile of boulders, casually scanning the area.

It annoyed the hell out of Slade. He'd had his men positioned among the boulders for the past ten minutes. The plan was for two other men on the far side of the trail, up on top of the cliff, to roll some big rocks over the edge and block the trail. Then, when the people with the wagons had all their attention ahead, he and the men in the boulders would hit them from the side. They should be able to get the drop on them, maybe without any shooting, then take the money and run. "Shoot," he said to Dante, who was standing next to him. "That bastard's gonna screw up all the timing. If he sees us in here . . ."

"Ah, you worry too much," Dante said. He picked up his

rifle, and before Slade knew what he intended, raised it, and shot the guard out of his saddle.

"Well that cuts it, boys," Slade called out to his men. "Let's hit 'em!" A moment later a dozen men were riding toward the wagons, hastily pulling up bandannas to cover their lower faces. The men in the train had been alerted by the killing of the guard. The other guard started to raise his rifle, but Dante, having spurred past Slade, put two rifle bullets into the man's chest.

Few of the men with the wagons fought back. John Simpson was an exception. Reaching behind the wagon seat, he pulled out a double barreled shotgun and fired one barrel at a man rushing his wagon. He missed. The huge boom of the shotgun caused the bandit to swerve to one side, seeking easier prey.

The bandits were among the wagons now, firing into them. One of the drivers went down, hit in the shoulder. Milton Duval rode straight at another wagon, and when the driver was slow about raising his hands, shot him three times with his Winchester, killing the man instantly. "Just so you don't have all the fun, Dante," he shouted across to his brother.

Meanwhile, another of the bandits charged straight at John Simpson's wagon. Simpson had the breach of his shotgun open as he shoved in fresh shells. Seeing the shotgun, and excited by all the shooting, the man snapped a shot at Simpson. The bullet took Simpson high in the shoulder, knocking him off his seat, but as he fell, he took the shotgun with him. The bandit rode around the wagon, saw Simpson lying on the ground, and rode straight at him. Simpson, stunned by the shock of the bullet and the impact against the ground, was regaining his senses. He raised the shotgun, aimed it up at the bandit, who was about to ride his horse right over him, and touched off both barrels. The double load of shot took the man in the lower abdomen, angling upwards, tearing a great hole in his body. The only reason the man didn't fall was that he had the reins wrapped around his right hand, and in his dying moments he managed to hold on as his horse ran off to the side. The animal had been struck by a few of the pellets and, crazy with pain, ran for twenty yards before its rider finally tumbled off the horse's back, hitting the ground dead.

Meanwhile, Simpson, realizing the shotgun was empty and in pain from his shoulder wound, knew he was a dead man if he couldn't find some way to get the out of the open. For the moment, he was sheltered by the wagon, but that wouldn't help him for long. There was a shallow gully by the side of the trail, formed by storm water channeling off the cliff. Simpson tossed the shotgun under the wagon, then rolled into the gully. He heard more shooting behind him, and scrambled on his hands and knees along the little gully, heading toward a point where it grew deeper and choked with weeds. He hid himself as best he could.

The three surviving drivers stood up on their wagon seats, with their hands in the air. "We got 'em, boys" Slade shouted. "It's all over."

It wasn't over. To Slade's surprise, Dante rode up to one of the wagons and shot the driver in the head.

"Hey!" Slade called out to Dante. "I said it was over!"

"Uh-uh," Dante called back. "They seen Milton's face, and he called out my name. We can't let any of them get back and start yappin'."

Dante was already riding toward another of the surrendered drivers. The man raised his hands higher and called out, "For God's sake, Mister. I won't—"

It was too late. Dante fired again, hitting the man in the chest. The man fell off the wagon seat and onto the ground. Dante rode closer, and aiming down, shot the man dead. "It's gotta be done, Slade," Dante shouted.

That son of a gun, Slade thought angrily, *calling out my name that way so I can't do anything but let him go ahead and kill 'em all.* He glanced over toward Milton, saw that indeed he had not had the common sense to pull up his bandanna. Slade cursed under his breath. Where had he ever gotten the stupid idea of bringing along the Duval brothers? *Loco*, both of them—just plain *loco*.

Now Dante went after the remaining driver who, seeing death riding his way, scooted back into the interior of the wagon, fumbling among the cargo for the rifle he'd thrown away. Dante opened fire as he rode at the wagon, half a dozen rounds from his Winchester, firing through the canvas cover. The driver, hit in the back and hip, rolled out into the open, screaming in pain. Dante, smiling, put three more rounds into him. The man clung onto the wagon seat for a moment, then fell to the ground and died.

They were all dead now, the drivers and the guards— except for John Simpson, hugging the ground in his little gully, hoping the bushes covered him well enough. His mind was full of the sounds of his men dying at the wagons. *Murderers*, he thought, *murdering scum*. He knew the Duval brothers by sight, had seen them around town often enough, usually with their brother, the sheriff. Then, they'd made him nervous. Now, they terrified him. If he lived through this, if they didn't ride over here and find his hiding place, if he survived to make it back to town, he'd see that they paid. He'd see them hang.

Chapter Sixteen

John Simpson lost track of time as he lay in the gully. He was vaguely aware that the noise from the direction of the wagons was diminishing. There were a last few calls among the bandits. "Whoo-eeee. What a mess," one man cried out disgustedly. Then there was a pounding of many hooves, which quickly faded away into the distance.

Still, John Simpson lay in the gully, unmoving. They might come back. They might see him if he stood up now. He was not certain he could move. His wounded shoulder throbbed dully, his entire body felt weak, helpless. What finally got him moving was the realization that he was losing blood, and that if he lay here long enough, he'd bleed to death.

It took Simpson a full five minutes to work his way out of the gully. He moved on hands and knees at first, which caused his shoulder to hurt so badly that he finally stood up, then staggered up over the rim of the gully.

There was not a person in sight, not a living person anyway. He could see one man hanging half out of one of the wagons, his blood running in a wide smear down the wooden side. Simpson went from wagon to wagon, looking for signs of life but found none. They were all dead—

six men, including the two guards. Simpson went to his own wagon and held onto the side for a moment, sick, dizzy, weak. Finally forcing himself up into the box, letting his wounded arm trail, he dug out the small chest in which he kept medicines and salves, mostly for treating the horses. There were strips of clean linen. He wrapped one around the wound in his shoulder, placing a thick pad of linen against the wound itself. Using his good arm and his teeth, he eventually got the makeshift bandage knotted in place.

Then he drank, deep gulps from one of the water jugs fixed to the side of the wagon, splashing some of the water over his face. He briefly considered burying the dead men. No, that was crazy. He didn't have the strength. He would have to use whatever energy he had left to get someplace where his wound could be treated. Blood was already staining the bandage. He needed help, and he needed it quickly. He would have to leave the dead where they lay, send back people to bury them properly. Until then, their only care would come from the buzzards and coyotes.

Simpson crawled up onto the wagon seat and picked up the reins, intending to get the horses moving, but the movement sent such a jolt of pain through his shoulder that he nearly fainted. There was no way he would be able to drive an entire team using only one arm.

He slid down from the seat again. Where were the guards' horses? There was one about a hundred yards away, cropping grass near the place where its rider had been shot from the saddle—no sign of the other guard's horse, maybe the bandits had taken it with them.

For the next ten minutes Simpson tried to coax the horse close to him. The animal, spooked by the earlier gunfire and made uneasy by the smell of Simpson's blood, refused to come nearer. When Simpson walked toward it, lurching unsteadily, the horse shied away. He got within twenty yards, then the horse, with a snort of fear and disgust, broke into a trot, and in a few seconds had disappeared around a bend in the trail.

Simpson went back to the wagons. It took him half an hour to unhitch one of the team horses from his own wagon, a horse he knew well—a steady, patient animal. The horse wrinkled its nose at the blood smell, but eventually Simpson had it unhitched. He'd have to ride the animal bareback, if he could even mount. Finally, leading the horse next to the wagon, Simpson got up onto the seat, then stepped across onto the horse's back.

During the long ride, Simpson's mind flickered in and out of consciousness. He fought to concentrate. He guided the horse using only his knees, with the fingers of his good arm tangled in its mane. Several times he nearly fell off, but managed to catch himself. He knew that if he fell, he would probably not be able to remount. He'd die on the trail from loss of blood.

Simpson had at first considered heading for the mine. Then he realized that the town was actually closer, and that the town had a doctor. So he took his slow, meandering way into town. He was still two miles shy of his goal when a party of men, riding in from the range, found him. One of the men knew him. "John!" the man shouted when he finally recognized the blood-stained figure slumped over the horse's neck. "What happened?"

Simpson was almost beyond words. "Dead," he managed to murmur. "All dead. Every man Jack."

The men escorted him the rest of the way in, propping him up from each side. They naturally attracted attention as they rode down the main street, heading for the doctor's house. By then the men had gotten a few more words out of Simpson. "Bandits hit the mine supply train," one man shouted out to a slowly growing crowd. "Killed ever'body but old John, here."

Word eventually reached the law—not the sheriff at first; few now had any trust in the sheriff's ability, or interest, in doing anything about the bandits who infested the territory. As usual, Jack Kerson was in the saloon, dealing cards. Clay was with him. A man came rushing into the saloon and came straight to the marshal's table. "Killed 'em all," the man burst out. "Killed 'em in cold blood."

"What are you blatherin' about?" Kerson demanded. "Calm down and . . ."

"The mine wagon train," the man replied. "Bandits killed everybody 'ceptin' for old John Simpson. He's over at the doctor's now, shot up real bad."

Kerson was on his feet, heading toward the doorway. "Come on," he called back to Clay, who, scooping up the money but leaving the cards where they lay, followed Jack out the door.

At first, the doctor would not let them talk to Simpson. "I've got to get the bullet out of his shoulder," he insisted, "and get him resting a little. Then you can ask all your questions."

So it was another half an hour before Simpson got a chance to tell his story. By then Mark and Luke had shown up and, with Jack, were crowding around Simpson's bed. The room was half-full of other men, all pushing in as close as the doctor would let them, hanging on every word. Clay stood back in a corner, listening. "Damn!" Jack said when Simpson was most of the way through with his account of the robbery. "You sure it was Dante and Milton? Stone sure?"

"No mistake about it," Simpson insisted. Now that he had the chance to tell what had happened, some of his strength was returning. "Saw Milton's face. Heard 'em calling to each other. Slade was there, too. It was his gang. Those Duval scum . . . riding from wagon to wagon, killin' unarmed men in cold blood. Animals!"

There was a sudden stir by the door. The crowd parted, and Henry Duval shouldered his way through the crowd. Every eye turned on him—and every eye was cold, accusing.

"What's going on here?" he demanded. "Why wasn't I told . . . ?"

Jack turned to face him. "I guess nobody wanted you to have a chance to cover this up, Duval. This is one you can't sweep under the rug."

"What are you talking about, Kerson?"

A cold smile creased Jack's lips. "Those two brothers of yours. The poets. Seems they got caught red-handed. They were seen doing their killing. There's an eye witness, and no way you can save their skins this time."

Jack curtly told Duval about the raid on the wagon train the killings and that his brothers had been identified by the lone survivor. "Bull!" the sheriff burst out. "Let me have a talk with him that lying old goat."

"You stay the hell away from me, Duval. You an' those two murderin' brothers o' yers. I ain't' gonna give you the time o' day," Simpson said.

Duval tried to push closer to Simpson, but the men in the room had grown hostile. "You leave him alone, Sheriff," one man snarled. "Ain't you Duvals done enough to him? Bunch o' murderin' . . ."

Duval was actually pushed out of the room, and as he went out the door, he could hear John Simpson calling weakly after him. "I'll see 'em hang. When I was layin' there, listenin' to 'em murder my men, I swore I'd see 'em hang."

Duval cursed under his breath, his face flaming with rage. Once out in the street, he forced himself to think. He had no doubt that Kerson would go straight to the judge, demanding a warrant. The sheriff headed for the judge's house. It was growing dark. He took back alleys, not wanting to be seen. After he pounded on the door for a while, the judge finally let him in. "What the hell, Duval? What's all that ruckus I heard a while ago?"

Duval pushed in past the judge. "Trouble. Those damned Kersons are at it again, claiming my brothers shot up a wagon train. The only witness is an old coot, John Simpson, and he's half out of his head with loss of blood. We can discount . . ."

"What?" the judge demanded. "Well, I know old John. He's the most truthful man I ever met. If he said . . . if you can't control those two brothers of yours . . ."

Duval stepped closer to the judge, grabbed him by the front of his shirt and yanked him close, glaring into the other man's face. "Why . . . you damned . . ."

For a moment he saw fear in the judge's face, then it was replaced by stubbornness. "Duval," the judge said. "This isn't any good. I've helped you cover up for those boys in the past, hoped you'd get 'em under control, but there's a limit. Somebody's gonna have the brains to bypass me and run to the circuit court. Then a lot of things are gonna come out. How you and me . . ."

Anger flared inside Duval. For a moment he considered pulling out his gun and pistol-whipping the judge. He actually got as far as wrapping his fingers around the pistol's butt, then, with a visible effort, he controlled himself, realizing he was not thinking clearly. However, he was rewarded by the return of a spark of fear in the judge's eyes—maybe he could control him for a little while longer. "There's no point in us standing here talking," he said. "We're wasting time."

Duval became aware of a growing noise outside, the murmur of many voices and an occasional shout. He turned toward a window, noticing a flickering glare. He pulled back the drapes a little. A mob was forming, several of them holding torches. In the torchlight he caught sight of Jack Kerson, standing with both his brothers. Kerson started toward the judge's front door.

"God!" the judge burst out, looking over the sheriff's shoulder. "You can see, Henry! Can't you see? I'll have to issue a warrant. I'm an elected official. I . . ."

Duval pushed the judge away from the window. "Get your coat," he snarled.

"What?" the judge bleated.

Duval walked over to where the judge's coat hung from a coat rack, picked it up and threw it at him. "Put it on. We're going out the back door. Let that bunch of clowns shout and stomp. You won't be here to dance to their tune. We'll hole up over at my place tonight. Won't nobody dare . . ."

"What'll we gain . . . ?"

"Time," Duval snarled, pushing the judge—who was holding his coat against his stomach—toward the back door. "Time to think."

There was one last flare of resistance from the judge. "Think, Henry? I guess that's something you haven't been doing much of lately—not since those two brothers of yours showed up."

Chapter Seventeen

The sun rose the next morning on a town filled with tension. The mob of the night before had dispersed and the judge was still hidden at the sheriff's house, but a mood of smoldering anger had taken hold of the population. Jack Kerson and his two brothers arrived at the marshal's office not long after sunup. Jack plunked himself down in his chair. "Damned judge," he snarled. "He's gutless."

"We know where he is," Luke replied. "Let's just go over to Duval's house and drag him out."

"I don't think we can do that," Jack said. "It'd be better to forget the warrant and just go after the gang, like we did before. If we find Dante and Milton with them . . ."

"Yeah, what's all this legal stuff, anyhow?" Mark asked.

"It's just to make sure they can't weasel out of it again." Jack said. "Let's go get us some breakfast."

The three men lingered over their breakfasts, talking occasionally about the raid on the supply wagons, but they didn't want to say too much in the restaurant. Although the town was stirred up, there were still factions. So, they all traipsed over to the marshal's office, where Jack seated himself once again in his chair. "We gotta figure out who we can count on to ride with us when we go after Slade."

"Clay, for sure," Mark said, "and I can think of a few more. There are a lot of men, who won't have to guts to tangle with Slade's bunch. We don't know how many of them there actually are. Does anybody even know where they hole up after a raid?" They talked for another hour, trying to figure the best way to go after the bandits. Mark suggested going to the territorial government, maybe enlisting the aid of the U.S. Marshal's office.

"Naw," Jack said. "Then Henry Duval could interfere, slow things down, and his precious brothers would have time to skedaddle. They may have already left the territory. We have to go after them ourselves. The time'll never be better. People are fed up with this situation. They . . ."

There was the sound of boot heels pounding along the boardwalk in their direction, someone moving fast. A man burst into the office. "Marshal," he said tersely, "I thought you better know . . . Slade just rode into town with a few of his boys."

Three pairs of boots came off desks and slammed down onto the floor. Three pairs of eyes fastened onto the man, who, sensing the drama of the moment, finally added: "Dante and Milton Duval are with him. They all rode into town bold as brass, and right at this moment are over at Jack Smith's saloon."

Jack jumped up from his chair. "What the hell's got into them? Do they think the sheriff can protect them after what they did?"

"Maybe they don't realize that we know," Luke said. "John Simpson said Dante and Milton rode from wagon to wagon, killing the men so's there wouldn't be any witnesses. Maybe they don't know Simpson survived and made it back to town. They think they're home free."

"Maybe," Jack said. "Maybe that's it. Maybe they just don't know." His face hardened. "If that's the way it is, they've made a big mistake. A mistake that's gonna kill 'em.

'Cause they're dead men. Every damned one of them. Mark, go out and see of you can find Clay."

Luke had guessed correctly. Nobody in Slade's gang had the slightest idea that anyone even knew the wagon train had been ambushed, and certainly not who had done the ambushing. True, Slade had been against coming into town at all—at least not Jack Kerson's town—but the Duval brothers, with a lot of money in their pockets, were feeling their oats. Money was for spending, and if the Kerson brothers got in the way, too bad for the Kersons. Their enthusiasm spread to other men in the gang. Seven men road into town together, feeling secure in their numbers. There were Slade and the Duvals, and four of Slade's men.

They headed straight for Jack Smith's saloon, their usual watering place, and immediately began to make up for the lack of whiskey at the hideout. At first they noticed nothing, although the bartender could not meet their eyes. There had been a few other men inside the saloon when Slade's bunch first arrived, but they began to drift out the door, one by one, looking back nervously at the bandits. Slade, whose sharp eyes had so far kept him alive, noticed. "What's the matter with everybody?" he muttered to Dante.

Dante grinned. "Guess we make people nervous."

Milton overheard. "Damned right we do." He, too, grinned. The last man in the bar who was not a part of the gang started to brush by him, heading toward the door. Milton grabbed the man by the arm. "What's the matter?" he asked. "Kinda jumpy today?"

The man muttered something, shook loose, and continued on toward the door. "Hey!" Milton shouted after him. "I was talkin' to you, Mister!"

The man was already passing through the door; he shied to one side as someone else pushed past him into the saloon. Much to Slade's surprise, the man was Henry Duval. "Well, howdy, Sheriff," Slade said, hiding his dislike of Duval behind a grin, but the grin faded when Duval burst out, "What's the matter with you? Have you gone completely crazy?"

"What you yappin' about?" Slade demanded angrily. "I don't like . . ."

"That wagon train—you hold it up, kill six men, then ride into town like a bunch of idiots? I . . ."

"How'd you know about us and the wagons?" Slade asked, then caught himself. "Sheriff, you know everybody's always trying to tie a can to our tails. We didn't have nothin' to do with . . ."

"There was a witness," the sheriff said bluntly. "The wagon boss has been spreading the story all over town."

Duval swung toward his brothers, who were both leaning against the bar holding glasses of whiskey. Milton's eyes widened a little, Dante's expression didn't change at all. Milton spoke up. "Henry, there weren't no witnesses left. Somebody's lyin'. We took care of 'em all."

The sheriff looked around quickly, but no one had overheard—no one was in sight; even the bartender had disappeared. The sheriff spun to face Slade. "Why did you get my brothers involved in this?" he snarled.

It was Dante who answered. "We're big boys, Henry. We decide what we do."

"We were out of money," Milton put in. "Stone broke. The only reason we came to this dump was because you told us about all the easy pickins. So we been out pickin'."

"Well, the next thing you're gonna do is pick up and move right on out of here. The whole town is in an uproar. It wouldn't surprise me if Jack Kerson leads a lynch mob over here."

Dante spoke again, his voice cold. "That's all I ever hear from you, Henry . . . Jack Kerson. Sounds like he's got you buffaloed. You twitch every time his name comes up," he looked straight at his brother, "but he ain't got me buffaloed."

"Me neither," Milton said. "I think it's time we had it out with those yahoos."

There was an answering growl from the other men in the room. "Seven against three," Slade said. "I think Milton's right. It's time we had it out with the Kersons." Slade was still smarting from the number of his men who'd already been killed or driven out of the area by the marshal and his brothers.

"Think?" the sheriff demanded angrily. "You call that thinking? The town's at a slow boil. The odds might not be as good as you think."

"Naw," Slade growled. "These townies ain't got the guts. They'll grouse and moan, but they'll stay out of it."

"Parker won't," the sheriff said. "He'll stand with the Kersons because Milton killed the Johnson kid. Seven to four might not be such good odds after all."

"That Parker," Dante said, "I want a piece of him. I don't know how he got everybody so buffaloed, but he's like any other man. He can go down."

The sheriff started to say something again, but had second thoughts. Maybe this wasn't such a bad thing after all. Even if Slade and his brothers rode out peacefully, the killings at the wagon train had probably lost him his chance of re-election . . . unless he could apply pressure, make sure the vote came out the way he wanted. He could never do that if the Kersons were still around. Yes, maybe it would be best to let Slade and his brothers take care of the Kerson bunch once and for all. Then he'd be top dog again, the way he'd been before the Kersons showed up, but it had to look right.

"Okay," he said, "but don't go out looking for them. Let 'em come to you. There isn't any warrant; I took care of that. If they do come after you and start shooting, they'll be in the wrong. You'll just be protecting yourselves. As for that wagon boss, maybe he'll die from his wounds. I'll go ahead and make sure he does, maybe later today." He started toward the door.

"Hey, where you goin'?" Slade demanded. "You ain't gonna stand with us?"

"Use your head," Duval snapped. "I want to make this all legal. I gotta be seen tryin' to stop it. I'm gonna go over, corral the judge and get him to issue some kind of injunction against the Kersons—put them squarely on the wrong side of the law."

Standing in the doorway, he looked back into the saloon, surprised to see an expression on Dante's face that looked almost like contempt. That rocked him for a moment, but he knew he was right. He had to plan for the future. This had to be done legally. He turned and went out the door.

While the Slade gang continued to soak up whiskey inside the saloon, other forces were gathering across town. Mark had not had to go for Clay; he showed up at the marshal's office as Mark was starting out the door. "Just heard that Slade's bunch is in town," Clay said to Jack.

"Yep," Jack replied in a totally flat voice.

"You going after them?" Clay asked, just as flatly.

"Yep." A slight hesitation. "And you . . . ?"

"Count me in. I'll go back to the hotel and get my rifle."

"No rifles," Jack said. "We don't want to go walking through town looking like the army. Later, people could say . . ."

There must still be no warrant, Clay thought. So it would be just a personal confrontation. That was fine with him. He had a score to settle with the Duvals, and didn't need any legal trappings, had never needed any kind of outside permission to justify his actions. On the other hand, he hated facing a mob like Slade's with just the pistol he wore on his hip. No man in his right mind would choose a pistol over a rifle. "You got an extra gun?" he asked Jack.

The marshal opened a drawer. Two pistols lay inside. Clay picked one up, tested the action, then opened the loading gate and began shoving rounds into the cylinder. When the pistol was loaded, he shoved it into his belt. He had a dozen rounds before he would need to reload. He watched Luke walk over to the gun rack and lift out a sawed-off shotgun. Luke slid a couple of rounds into the breech, then clicked the gun shut. "I'll carry it under my coat," he told Jack.

Jack hesitated a moment, then nodded. As for his own armament, he put on his long linen duster, then dropped a pistol into each of the side pockets. Mark did the same, shrugging into a coat that sagged a little with the weight of the pistols. The four men glanced at one another. "Let's go do it," Jack said.

They clumped out onto the boardwalk and, with a nod from Jack, started in the direction of Smith's saloon—four big men, the Kersons wearing their dusters, Clay a short denim jacket, one pistol on his hip and another thrust into his belt, the walnut grips gleaming softly in the morning light.

There were few people in the street; the whole town had by now heard about Slade's arrival. There was no doubt there would be a showdown. Those few who encountered the marshal's group stepped off the boardwalk and vanished into doorways. One man, after a startled look, turned and sprinted away. "One of Henry Duval's toadies," Jack said softly. "Probably gone to warn him."

"What do we do if the sheriff shows up?" Mark asked.

"If he gets in the way, if he sides with his brothers and Slade, we treat him the same as them."

There were no more questions. The saloon was now in sight. The four men moved off the boardwalk and into the street. Two of Slade's men were seated in the chairs on the boardwalk in front of the saloon's doorway. When they spotted the Kersons and Clay, one went inside the saloon. A moment later, the saloon's double doors swung open. The man came out again, with Slade, and Dante and Milton Duval close behind. Two more men joined them. Now seven men stood together on the boardwalk. "Good," Clay said to Jack. "They're bunched up. Let's spread out, make them hunt for targets."

Just at that moment, Henry Duval turned the corner at the far end of the street and saw Jack Kerson's group standing in the middle of the street, facing the men on the boardwalk. The sheriff felt a twinge of alarm. The Kersons were well spread out, with several feet separating each of them, while Slade's men formed a milling mass in front of the saloon. "Spread out, you idiots," he muttered, then started down the street. He was beginning to wonder if this should be happening. He'd just spent a frustrating half an hour with the judge, who, to Duval's amazement, had held firm. "What do you mean, injunction?" the judge had whined. "There's no cause for anything like that. Just get those brothers of yours out of town."

When the shooting began, Henry Duval was too far away to interfere—but he saw and heard the whole thing.

Milton called out, "Parker! You son of a horned toad. . . ."

"Jimmy Johnson, Duval," Clay said to Milton. "It's time to pay for that boy's life."

"Screw you, Parker."

"A life for a life," Clay said.

Milton looked around at the men on either side, at his brother Dante. He grinned. "Big talk, Parker." Then he made the mistake of looking Clay straight in the eyes, and all his bravado cracked and froze in those icy depths.

"Draw," Clay said. "Or I'll kill you where you stand."

"You rotten . . . !" Milton screamed, his voice high and wavering.

"Draw," Clay repeated, taking a half-step toward Milton.

Now Dante interfered. "Cool down, Milton," he murmured. "You heard Henry . . . let them start it."

"Damn it, let's spread out," Slade said at almost the same time. "We're all bunched up . . ."

Milton barely heard either men. He could not break his

gaze away from Clay's. He saw the cold implacable purpose in Clay's eyes and knew that Clay would do it, would simply draw his pistol and kill him. "Aaahhh!" Milton screamed, clawing for his pistol.

He's fast, Clay realized, *but wild.* Milton fired first, but Clay shifted a little to one side. The bullet flew a foot wide. Then Clay drew, his pistol suddenly in his hand, flame spurting from the muzzle. The first bullet took Milton low on the right side of his chest, driving him backwards . . . right into two men bunched behind him. He still held his pistol, but was flailing with his left hand, struggling for balance, his arm knocking aside the gun hand of the only one of Slade's men who had, so far, drawn a gun. He staggered against Dante.

Clay moved forward, cocking his pistol. "For the boy," he said, firing another bullet into Milton Duval, this time hitting him in the stomach.

An inarticulate cry burst from Dante Duval as he saw the second bullet fold his brother almost double. He clawed his pistol free and aimed it at Clay, who was once again ready to fire at Milton—but Mark had his pistol out now, and shot Dante in the left arm, the bullet plowing a furrow through the muscle, spinning Dante halfway around and further adding to the tangle on the boardwalk.

"Spread out!" Slade repeated, this time shouting. He had his pistol in his hand and snapped a shot at Jack Kerson, but by now Luke had swung the shotgun out from beneath his coat and cocked one of the big hammers. The shotgun bellowed, sending most of the huge pellets into Slade's torso, although a few of them, missing Slade, tore into two of his men.

By now the firing was general, deafening. The men on the boardwalk had finally untangled themselves enough to bring up their pistols, but they were so rattled that their shooting was wild. Jack Kerson shot one of them through the head, while Luke discharged the second barrel of his shotgun into another.

The boardwalk was a scene of carnage: Slade was down, already dead or dying, his chest a bloody ruin. Milton Duval was still on his feet, his pistol still in his right hand, but he was bent nearly double, his legs sagging from the weight of the two bullets already in his body. Dante Duval, his left arm streaming blood, had been knocked off balance again by the second man Luke had shotgunned. Jack Kerson shot another of Slade's men, hitting him in the throat, and Luke was firing at the single man on the boardwalk who had not been hit.

There had been a continuous roar of gunfire, but now there was a lull. Milton straightened up and raised his pistol in Clay's direction. "Parker," he called out.

"Right here," Clay answered. "For the boy, Duval."

Clay fired one more shot, this time hitting Milton in the center of his chest. Milton flew straight backwards, landing flat on his back. "Milt!" Dante cried out, an anguished shout. He started to aim at Clay, but saw that Luke had just reloaded his shotgun and was in the act of snapping the breach closed. In another moment those two barrels would be tracking onto him. He raised his pistol and fired quickly, his bullet hitting Luke low in the body. As Luke fell, the shotgun roared, the load of buckshot splintering wood next to Dante, one of the pellets nicking him on the side of the face.

Now he was the only one of Slade's bunch still in condition to fight; the man Mark had been firing at had run back into the saloon. Dante sensed the attention of all his opponents focusing onto him. Jack Kerson fired a shot at him, while Mark began to aim. Clay was looking toward where Milton had fallen. "Damn you to hell!" Dante screamed, snapping a single shot toward Clay, but bullets were now singing all around him. He jumped backwards in a controlled fall, vanishing through the swinging doors and into the darkness of the saloon.

No one followed Dante. Mark and Jack were bent over Luke, who was lying half on one side, his face white with pain and shock, blood pooling beneath his lower body. Clay started toward the saloon, but Jack stopped him. "You'll be framed against the outside light," he warned. By then it was too late; the sound of a horse being run hard came from the alley behind the saloon. "He's gone," Jack said.

Henry Duval reached the scene of the fight. He moved straight to where Milton lay, knelt beside him. "Milt," he said, trying to raise his brother's head. For a few seconds there was a flicker of recognition in Milton's eyes, "Help . . . me," he murmured. Then his eyes went blank.

The sheriff continued to hold his brother's head up for a few more seconds, then tried to lay it down gently, but his fingers slipped and Milton's head thudded heavily onto the dirty boardwalk. The sheriff stood up slowly, his face dead white. Turning, he faced Clay. "I saw you shoot my brother," he said. "I saw you gun him down."

Clay stood facing Duval, his face expressionless. "A life for a life," he finally said. "His for the boy he killed. Your brother was a wild animal, Duval."

"Yes . . . a life for a life," the sheriff said woodenly, then more animation came into his voice. "Remember that, Parker. A life for a life. Your life for my brother's."

"Anytime you think you can collect, Duval. Right here and now . . . if that's the way you want it." Clay's hand moved toward the pistol thrust into his belt.

The sheriff looked as if he was going to reach for his own pistol. Then, with a visible effort, he got hold of himself. "No, Parker. Later. When you don't expect it. When you won't know where it's coming from." The sheriff turned and walked away.

Clay watched him go, then realized that Jack was calling to him. "Give us a hand. We got to get Luke to the doc's. He's hit pretty bad."

Clay watched Henry Duval vanish out of sight around a corner, then turned toward the boardwalk. No sign of movement there, just five bodies, blood soaking into the splintered planking. *My God*, he thought, *this town is a slaughter-house*. He shook his head, then moved toward where Mark and Jack were bent over Luke.

Two blocks away, Henry Duval moved along the street like a sleepwalker. He stopped at a door beneath a sign that read: UNDERTAKER. He rapped hard on the door. It opened quickly. A skinny man wearing a black coat stood in the doorway, smiling obsequiously. *He knows*, Duval thought. *He's heard the shooting. He knows there's going to be plenty of business today*. Duval felt a surge of hatred, wanted to blast that smarmy smile off the man's face. Instead, he gave curt orders for Milton's burial.

Duval turned away while the undertaker was still smiling; he had to get out of there, had to walk. He noticed that the streets, which had been deserted only minutes before, were now filling with people, many of them no doubt heading for Jack Smith's saloon to gawk at the bodies, to stare at Milton's dead body.

The rage returned. That Parker . . . no, Jack Kerson. The marshal had been a thorn in Duval's side ever since the three Kerson brothers had first shown up in town. They'd pay. Every last one of them would pay, including Parker. He was tempted to head back to the saloon and start shooting, but he knew they'd kill him without hesitation.

Duval started toward his house and saw the judge walking rapidly along the street toward him. "What was all that shooting about?" the judge blurted, stopping a few feet away, his face working nervously.

Duval's rage began to grow again, and at last here was an object on which he could vent that rage. "The shooting?" he replied, his voice quiet, but mocking. "That little bit of shooting? That was just the Kerson brothers and Parker killing my little brother."

"My God, Henry," the judge stammered. "That's awful."

"Yeah, ain't it," Duval said, his voice a little tighter now.

"You couldn't see your way to issuing that injunction. You had to buck me."

"Henry," the judge said, his voice rising nervously, "I told you why I couldn't . . ."

Duval felt the rage swelling inside him as he remembered the way Milton's head had thudded down onto the board-walk, remembered the look of horror that had been frozen forever in his brother's dead eyes. Looking straight at the judge, he began to pull his pistol from its holster. "I told you never to buck me," he said, his voice rising just a little, but still relatively calm. His pistol was now in his hand. He pulled back the hammer, aimed at the judge.

"Henry!" the judge shouted, his face white with fear. "What are you doing? Have you lost your mind?"

"My brother's dead," Duval said, "and so are you."

One last cry from the judge, then Duval opened fire. The first two bullets knocked the judge down onto his back in the street. He was still alive, staring up in horror at Duval. "You're dead," Duval snarled, and emptied the pistol into the judge's body.

Ten minutes later, Henry Duval had saddled his horse and was riding out of town.

Chapter Eighteen

After the gunsmoke died down, the town's balance of power shifted considerably, but not in quite the manner Jack Kerson had expected. Milton Duval was dead, and Henry and Dante Duval were on the run. However, Luke was badly injured—so badly that it soon became clear that he would never walk normally again. Dante's bullet had shattered his pelvis. He lay in bed day after day, gaunt and weak. "Nah, he probably ain't gonna die," the doctor told Jack, "but he's gonna be like this for a long time. It's hard to tell how long."

After all that gunfire, a goodly number of people in the town seemed to consider the Kersons as much a part of the region's problem as Slade and the Duvals. Most of the citizens shed no tears as the dead bandits were planted on Boot Hill, but at the same time, they were tired of gunplay, tired of lawmen who were quick on the trigger. They wanted peace.

Against Jack's advice, his brother Mark ran for sheriff. With Henry Duval a fugitive for killing the judge, Mark figured he could easily win the election, but to Mark's amazement and considerable disappointment, he lost badly. A man who had been running a small ranch took the election. A dour, no-nonsense man, who made it clear during the short campaign that the day of the gunfight was now over. He tolerated the Kersons, but was definitely not one of their supporters. "There ain't gonna be no personal vendettas in this county," he told Jack. "We'll do it by the book now. The law book."

When Mark heard of the conversation, he became enraged. "Why that slippery son of a gun!" he burst out. "We clean up the place for him, and he thinks he can just waltz in and . . ."

By now there was a new judge as well as a new sheriff. The judge was a stickler for law and order. The job of the two Kerson brothers deteriorated to keeping order in the town—locking up drunks, stopping fist fights.

Clay watched Jack and Mark fume. They were men who craved action, men who wanted to shape events. They had their own version of how the law should be enforced, and now the law seemed to be turning on them. A few friends of Henry Duval were demanding that the grand jury indict the Kersons and Clay for the killings in front of Jack Smith's saloon, which immediately stirred up various Kerson supporters. To head off trouble, the sheriff and the judge, working together, convinced the Grand Jury to delay the matter indefinitely. Discreet hints were made that perhaps, now that the bandit problem had been cleaned up, it was time for the Kersons to hit the road.

Clay was beginning to feel that might be the best idea for himself as well. He had seen Molly once since the gun fight. Her face had been like stone. All she said was: "You left two of them alive."

How hatred shrivels the soul, Clay thought as he walked back to his hotel.

Then word came that Henry and Dante Duval had gathered the survivors of the old Slade gang together. There were reports of robberies and killings way over at the far edge of the county. "Let that gutless sheriff handle it," Mark said. "When they run into enough trouble, they'll come to us, hat in hand."

They didn't. The new sheriff formed posses, and rode out to hunt down the new Duval gang. Usually they came back without having even sighted the bandits, but one time they got a little too close, and three of the posse members got shot up. Nobody was killed, but one man would never use his right arm again.

Still no call came for the aid of the Kersons. Instead, threats filtered in—threats against the marshal and his brothers. A note from Henry Duval, wrapped around a rock, was tossed through the window of the marshal's office. The note promised that the Kersons, and Clay, would die, and die hard. At the time, Jack and Mark were in the saloon, dealing cards. Someone came running, telling them about the broken window, but by then the horseman who'd thrown the stone was far away. The sheriff showed no inclination to pursue. In fact, he warned Jack Kerson to stay out of the county area.

Mark scoffed at the note. "Let the Duvals come. We'll blow 'em away."

Clay knew that Henry Duval was not about to let anyone get a fair shot at him, which was one of the reasons Clay did not leave. He longed to go, was more than ready to hit the trail, maybe ride on down south where it would be getting cold soon. With the town turning against the Kersons, however, he did not want to pull out on them—not until they finally got the idea on their own and left.

Luke couldn't be moved yet. He would have to have another two or three weeks of bed rest.

"Then I'll find a way to get him back home," Jack said.

Another reason Clay resisted leaving was because of the Johnson women—not so much Molly, but Jessica. She had decided to move back out to the mine. "It's home," she told Clay when he tried to dissuade her. Her men were buried out there, not far from the old house. "We'll be safe enough," she said. "There are a lot of men out there now—not just miners, guards, too. They're good men.

Clay wasn't sure how safe they'd actually be, but he was

impressed by a sense of steely determination that underlay Jessica's obvious sorrow. One afternoon, a week later, he saw the two women off; they left town in a wagon train loaded with new furnishings for the house, and several tons of mining equipment.

Clay and Molly had little to say to one another. She kissed him lightly on the cheek, a kiss with little warmth to it. Her eyes condemned him for leaving two of the Duval brothers alive. *The hell with it*, Clay thought. *I'm pulling out as soon as Jack and Mark ship Luke home.*

Then disaster struck. Jack and Clay were in the saloon, where Jack was dealing cards. There was just a single shot. "Sounds like it came from over on the next block," Clay said to Jack. Then they both heard the pounding of hooves, two horses being run hard. Jack seemed more annoyed than alarmed as he pushed back his chair and stood up. "Guess I better go check it out, unless Mark has already. . . ."

When Jack and Clay stepped out into the street, they heard shouting from the direction from which the shot had come, the area where the Kerson brothers rented a small frame house. "Where is Mark?" Jack said as they turned the corner . . . only to see several men crowding around the back of the Kerson house.

In that moment, Clay knew. He thought of trying to hold Jack back, but realized it would be no use. Jack seemed to have finally figured it out. He broke into a run toward the front door. In his haste, he kicked the door open and went racing inside, shouting. "Luke?"

Luke lay partway out of his bed, his eyes full of agony as he looked up at his older brother. "Heard it," Luke said weakly. "Couldn't do nothin' . . ."

They found Mark lying on the kitchen floor, dead. He'd been shot in the back, apparently as he sat at the kitchen table, eating a plate of beans and bacon. The kitchen window, which opened out onto an alley, was shattered.

It took only a few minutes before the story was put together. "It was them Duvals," one man said. "Henry and Dante. I seen 'em come racing outta the alley back there like their tails was on fire. They had their horses hitched around the corner, then took right off. I dived for cover. I figured if they seen me . . ."

Mark's funeral was a lonely affair. Very few mourners showed up at the rocky little cemetery outside town. Jack was there, of course, and Clay and half a dozen other men. That looked like it might be all, until, in the middle of the parson's jabbering, a buggy pulled up twenty yards away. Clay watched as the Johnson women, Jessica and Molly, stepped down from the buggy. They were dressed in the black they had worn when they buried their own men. Jack saw them coming and went over to open the rickety little gate that led into the cemetery. The service continued, the mourners standing together in a semicircle, heads down, until the coffin had been lowered into the ground, until the first shovelful of dirt began to rattle down onto the wood.

Jack went over to the two women. "Thanks for coming," he said to Jessica.

"We couldn't have done anything else," she replied.

"After all," Molly added, "they went down, yours and ours, fighting the same scum."

Clay glanced over at Molly, saw that the bitterness in her voice was echoed by the bleakness of her expression. Gone forever was the young, trusting, open youthfulness that had initially attracted him to the girl. Unfortunately, that freshness had not been replaced by a calm maturity—just the hardness, the anger and hatred that showed beneath the tautening skin of her face.

Molly saw Clay looking at her. She held his gaze for a moment, then glanced over at Jack. "Just tell me they won't get away with it," she said. Then she turned to follow her mother, who was already leaving the cemetery. Neither woman looked back.

The other men drifted away, while Jack and Clay watched the last of the dirt fill in Mark's grave. "No," Jack said.

Clay looked up. Jack turned toward him. "No, they won't get away with it," he said. "The girl's right. This thing isn't finished yet. It can't be. Not until . . ."

Clay followed Jack back to his house. Once inside, Jack shrugged off his somber mood, forced himself to smile at Luke, who smiled wanly back at him from his bed. "You feel up to traveling?" Jack asked his brother.

"Yeah, sure," Luke replied. "Just saddle up my old nag . . ."

"I was figurin' on something a little more comfortable," Jack said. "Yesterday I bought a wagon off old man Smith. That light one with the canvas top that you can fold up out of the way. As long as you gotta lie down, might as well do it inside a wagon. Soon we'll be on our way out to Los Angeles."

"We're going to Los Angeles?" Luke asked, his eyes lighting up.

"Yep. Wired Uncle Tod. He's headin' here with his clan. They're gonna take you and the wagon out to California."

"You goin', too?" Luke asked.

"Yeah, at least part of the way. Then maybe I'll ride off on my own for a while, take care of some unfinished business."

Luke looked up at his brother and nodded.

Tod Kerson showed up a week later. Like his brother, he was tall and rangy, with a set, no nonsense expression on his face. Tod was accompanied by his three sons, more chips off the same block of Kerson granite. Clay found himself thinking that if the whole Kerson clan had arrived together, this county would have been cleaned up a long time ago—or maybe it would have simply become a Kerson fief. He noticed how the entire town walked gingerly around the increased Kerson presence. Jack had told no one but Clay about the plan to move out to Los Angeles. "Don't want to let the wrong kinda people know we'll be out on the trail in a slow-moving wagon," he said, which made sense, even with Jack, Uncle Tod and his boys and Clay along to ride guard. "Care to ride along with us a ways?" Jack had asked him one day.

Clay wouldn't mind that at all. It was more than time to leave this town. There was nothing to hold him here. Sarah was gone, Molly out at the mine, where she showed every intention of staying. She almost never came into town now. She seemed to have sensed that all of her champions, the men most likely to avenge her father and brother, would soon be gone.

One day, two more men rode into town, hard-looking men. They immediately sought out Jack, who was, as usual, in the saloon with Clay. Jack introduced them to Clay as Pat and Tom. "We rode together a few years back," Jack explained. He did not elaborate, nor did Pat or Tom. Both men were heavily armed, and the way their eyes tested everything around them suggested they had at one time been hunters of men—perhaps occasionally the hunted themselves.

The day after Pat and Tom's arrival, the sheriff was gathering another posse, on a tip that the Duval gang had been seen near a big ranch on the far side of the county. "The poor dumb coot," Jack said. "Figures they're gonna wait around for him."

"Just another trick," Luke said from his bed. "They're doin' it again . . . sucking the law out of town."

"Naw," Jack replied. "We're still here. They wouldn't be dumb enough to hit the town with us . . ."

They were all gathered in the living room of the little house, the Kerson tribe, along with Clay. "Let 'em come," Luke called out; his bed was close to the bedroom door. "Just load up my old Greener an' prop me up by the front door. I'll give 'em both barrels."

"A nice thought," Jack said, "but we ain't gonna be here.

If they hit the town, let the town take care of it. We'll be long gone."

"We're leaving now?" Luke asked.

"Yep." Jack glanced over at his uncle. "Uncle Tod and me've been talking about it. Maybe this is the best time to go, while everyone's off in the boondocks chasing ghosts." He looked at Clay. "I know you've been chompin' at the bit. Can you be ready to ride at dawn?"

That was no problem at all for Clay. The next morning, even before the sky grew light in the east, the entire company was ready to ride. Luke was in the wagon, propped up on a mattress. A pair of mules had been hitched to the wagon, with one of Uncle Tod's boys doing the driving. Jack, Uncle Tod, his other two boys, Clay, and Pat and Tom were to ride mounted alongside. To Clay's surprise, a man named Jed was coming along, too—Clay had seen him around town, knew him as a local man, some kind of small rancher. All of the men were heavily armed.

Leaving so early, there was no one to see them off, except for an old man on his way to swamp out one of the saloons. Clay noticed that none of the Kerson group looked back as they drove out of town. Nor did he. He'd left too many places; looking back was a luxury he avoided.

By the time the sun was well above the horizon they were several miles west of town. They made their first stop at nine o'clock, at a little oasis where a small spring bubbled out of some rocks at the base of a slope, forming a pool about twenty feet across. The horses and mules immediately made for the pool, where the men tied the animals' reins to some stout bushes.

Clay went to the place where the spring water came out of the ground. He poured the stale town water from his canteen, then filled it with clear, cool spring water. He was bending down to take a drink when he noticed that the other men had gathered around the wagon, and were talking animatedly. Clay walked closer. He overheard Jack say: "I'd figured on following along with the rest of you for a day or two, but the sheriff riding out after the Duvals got me to thinking."

Jack looked up as Clay came close. "I figure it like this," he said. "For the moment, this Duval thing is gonna keep the sheriff busy and out of my hair. At the same time, the Duvals'll be occupied running the posse a wild goose chase. Nobody's gonna be looking for us. So I figure it's time to take care of that unfinished business."

Clay said nothing, just looked at Jack. "I know I got no right to ask you," Jack said, "but me, Pat, Tom, and Jed are gonna do a little hunting. We was wonderin' if you'd like to ride with us."

Clay had no doubt as to what, or who, these men would be hunting. He said nothing, simply mounted his horse when the others did. They all gathered around the wagon. Jack leaned down to speak to Luke. "Wish you could ride along, little brother."

"Yeah," Luke replied bleakly, propping himself up on one elbow.

A minute later the four men rode away from the wagon. Clay sat his horse for a moment, nodded down at Luke, then reined his horse around to follow the others. "Clay . . ." he heard Luke call out to him. Clay held back his horse, turned in the saddle to look back at Luke.

Clay . . ." Luke said. "It's . . . Jack . . . keep an eye on him for me."

Clay nodded, then spurred his horse away. Within a minute he had caught up with the others. Jack looked back once to where Uncle Tod and his boys stood around the wagon. "They'll see Luke safe to Los Angeles," he said. Then, turning his horse, he led the way northeast.

As they rode, Jack outlined his thinking to the others. "I figure the Duvals are gonna make some kinda false trail to confuse the sheriff, make him think he's actually gonna catch 'em, but the Duvals will probably circle around, maybe even get behind the posse. It's even possible they intend to raid the town, looking for me and Luke and Clay, or maybe they have something else in mind. The thing is, wherever the sheriff ends up is definitely not the place where the Duvals are gonna be."

Clay then discovered why Jed was along. His ranch had been burned out by the Slade-Duval gang. His wife had been killed in the attack. He was after revenge. "He knows the back areas of this county really well," Jack told Clay. "If anybody can figure out which way the Duvals are heading, it'll be Jed."

The ex-rancher guided them in a big loop that took them well to the northeast of town. "I figure the sheriff is ridin' more or less due east," he said. "We oughta cut his trail pretty soon."

They did; halfway through the afternoon they came on the tracks of a body of horsemen, heading east. "Figure they got half a day's start on us," Jed said. "Now, we lag back a little, see what we can find."

Two hours later, they discovered the tracks of another body of horsemen, coming in from the north. "See," Jed said. "They circled to the north, waited for the posse to pass on by, then cut south across their tracks."

"You figure it's the Duval bunch?" Pat asked Jed.

"Probably. Don't know of any other group of riders that'd be that big, except for the posse."

"So, where are they headed?" Jack asked.

"I ain't no fortune teller," Jed replied. "Just south."

Jack shrugged. "Guess maybe we oughta head south, too."

Chapter Nineteen

The tracks were easy to follow. They continued south. The five pursuers scanned the horizon for possible danger. Clay was the only one paying attention to the tracks themselves. In the middle of the afternoon he urged his horse over toward Jack. "Saw something," he said. "It's the tracks."

He pulled his horse around, went back down the trail a few yards. "Right here," he said, pointing at the ground. "Two sets of tracks branching off to the side."

"Yeah," Jack said. "I see it now. What . . . ?"

The other three men came riding over, and Clay told them about the tracks. "What's it mean?" Jed asked.

"Just that a couple of 'em took off on their own," Tom replied.

"I wonder," Jack mused aloud. "I just wonder if . . . well, there's two sets of tracks . . . so I wonder if Henry and Dante . . ."

"That'd cut it," Jed snorted.

"How old is this new trail?" Jack asked Clay.

"Real fresh. Whoever these two are, they angled away from the others only an hour or so ago."

It was decided that they would follow the two sets of tracks. For a while Jack had considered splitting up the group, with a couple of men following the new tracks, the rest continuing on after the main group. "Naw," he finally said. "We're few enough as it is, and we can always come back and pick up the main trail."

So all five men branched off to the west to follow the new tracks. They pushed their horses a little harder than was prudent; the two men they were following seemed to be taking their time, so they should come up to them soon.

Pushing that way, they found the two men without warning—a flicker of movement just fifty yards off the trail in a small copse of trees down by a stream bed. "Let's go, boys," Jack called out, and the five men rode hard for the trees, rifles sliding out of saddle scabbards. They heard a voice call out, "Jeez! It's the marshal!"

As the pursuers pounded down on the trees, they saw two men frantically mounting, each with a rifle out and ready. "I recognize one of 'em," Jack called out. "Saw him with Slade more than once."

The two men were clearly eager to get away, but they were trapped with a sheer cutbank behind them. Clay wondered if they'd have the brains to throw down their weapons, but they never had the chance. Jed raised his rifle, fired. One of the two men let out a yell, then fell over the rear end of his horse. The other raised his rifle in reflex, which was not a good move—Jack, Pat and Tom opened up with their own rifles. A storm of lead slammed the man out of his saddle. He hit the ground head first, rolled part way over, then did not move again.

By now the Kerson group was at the edge of the trees. Clay saw that the first man who'd been hit was still alive. He rose up onto his elbows. His rifle lay a yard away. Jed raised his own rifle, seemed about to put another bullet into the man. Clay crowded his horse close to Jed's, forced the barrel of the rifle upward. "Hold on," he snapped. "We need to talk to him."

The man on the ground held perfectly still as the five men

guided their horses close to where he lay. Pat slipped down out of his saddle, bent low and jerked the man's pistol out of its holster. He cocked the pistol, and held it aimed at the fallen man's head. The man's eyes, wide with fear, fastened on Pat.

While the others dismounted, Clay rode around the area in a circle, looking for the presence of any more men. He found nothing, expected nothing. When he rode back and dismounted, the others were gathered around the fallen man. Jack was down on one knee, bending low. Clay figured he must have been questioning the man. "Mike," the man was saying. "My name's Mike Armbruster. Me an' Zeke . . ." he looked over at the other man, who still had not moved, who was clearly dead. "Ah, you done gone an' killed Zeke. Shot him down like a dog. We was travelin' along all peaceful . . ."

"Forget the fairy tales, Armbruster," Jack snapped. "We followed you ever since you branched off from the others."

"Don't know about no others," Armbruster started to say. Then he began to cough and as he coughed, bright bubbles of blood formed at his lips. "Ah," he murmured. "You varmints have killed me, too. I'm lung shot."

"You were with the Duvals," Jack snapped. "You were riding with them."

Armbruster seemed about to deny it, then he slumped back, more bloody bubbles forming at his lips. "Those Duvals," he muttered, "crazy as loons . . ."

They pulled the blanket roll from Armbruster's horse, put it beneath his head. Tom tore Armbruster's shirt open. A bluish hole lay just a bit to the left of his sternum. Everyone, including Armbruster, could hear the air sucking in and out of the hole. "Ah," Armbruster said again. "Ah, damnit all."

They questioned him more gently after that. Tom pressed a wad of folded cloth over the bullet hole. Armbruster, knowing he probably didn't have much time left, talked quietly. "Me an' Zeke, we was fed up with the Duvals. Plum *loco*, they was, thinkin' about nothin' but revenge. We ain't made a big score since those two idiots took over the gang. Finally, this mine thing. That's real smart, hittin' a mine, not to get a payroll or anything—nothin' there for us. Maybe a little gold, but most of it still locked up in the ore."

"What?" Jack demanded. "What mine?"

"The Johnson place. Like I said, mostly for vengeance. They want to kill the Johnson women. Henry and Dante got somethin' against 'em. Well, Zeke an' me, we don't hold much with hurtin' women. So we faked trouble with our horses, got 'em to limp a little, and pulled off to the side, sayin' we'd follow on in a while, but we were figurin' to just keepin' on ridin' west."

Before Armbruster died, they got the rest of the story out of him. The gang would hit the mine at dawn the next day. Ride on in and see what there was to steal, but in Armbruster's opinion, just do a lot of killing. "They hate them women," Armbruster murmured just before he took his last breath. "Hate a lot of people. Stupid to ride with men all twisted up like that . . ."

It was nearly dark by then. They tumbled the bodies of Armbruster and Zeke to the base of the cutbank, then collapsed it down on top of them—enough, maybe, to keep away scavengers. To Clay, even that minimum burial took too much time. He wanted to get riding.

Jack had other ideas. "We know where they're heading. We know what they're gonna do, and we know when they're going to do it. What we need to do is ride on a ways, rest the horses, and rest us a little, too."

Clay had to admit that made good sense. They'd been pushing the horses pretty hard. The others all concurred. They rode on for another hour, until it grew too dark to see where they were going; the moon would not rise for several hours. They made a cold camp in the cover of some brush. The horses were staked out but not unsaddled. After feeding the animals some oats from a bag Jed had with him, the men lay down on their bedrolls.

As Clay lay down, Jack, whose bedroll was only a yard away, rolled over on his side, facing him. Clay could not make out Jack's features, could only detect the faint gleam of his eyes. "Tomorrow morning . . ." Jack said in a low, tense voice. "Tomorrow morning it's gonna end. Either for me, or for the Duvals, but whichever way it goes, they're gonna get a surprise they hadn't counted on . . ." There was a short silence. "That surprise is gonna be us."

The moon rose at two in the morning. After several minutes of grousing, stretching and spitting, and a few mouthfuls of hardtack and cold beef, the five men mounted, then headed southwest, toward the Johnson mine. They were still a mile short when it began to grow light. "Hold up," Jack called out. "We gotta find some cover. Scout the area. Find out where . . ."

He did not finish the sentence. A single shot boomed out from the direction of the mine. "Buffalo gun," Tom said.

The men listened intently. For ten or fifteen seconds there was no other sound. Then the sound of another shot, apparently from the same big-bore rifle. "Well," Pat put in, "sounds like the dance started without us."

A moment later there was the sound of several weapons being fired, a lighter, rolling series of pops. "Saddle weapons," Clay said, "probably the Duval bunch. It sounds like they didn't manage to surprise anybody. Those first two shots . . . a guard, maybe."

There was more shooting now, the reports all mixed together. "Let's get moving," Clay said. He spurred his horse forward. The others fell in behind him. After a few minutes of riding, they came to the back side of a ridge. From his trips to the Johnson mine, Clay knew that this ridge overlooked the mine area. He reined up, dismounting while his horse was still sliding to a stop. Reaching into his saddle bags, he pulled out his binoculars. A moment later he was on his belly at the edge of the rise, studying the land below.

The dawn light was growing quickly; the area around the mine stood out clearly. A group of perhaps a couple of dozen men were firing toward the mine buildings, from which rose a cloud of gunsmoke. In the soft light Clay could see flame flashing from the defenders' gun barrels.

Jack flopped down beside Clay. "Real dug in, those people at the mine," he said to Clay.

"Yeah, better than the Duvals."

The attackers had obviously been caught out in the open. Clay figured that they had probably tried to charge the mine even after they'd been spotted. Two bodies lay out in the open. The rest of the bandits were holed up behind what little cover they could find. Men crouched behind rocks, humps of dirt, anything. Several men were holding the horses back beyond the line of fire.

"Not much we can do right now," Jack said. Clay nodded. To get at the bandits, they'd have to cross a lot of open ground. The men with the horses would be able to take them from the side. Clay studied the men below carefully. "I think I see Henry Duval," he said, "up with the front line."

Jack snatched the glasses from him, scanned the whole scene below. "Yeah, he replied, "and I think that's Dante back with the horses. Hey . . . what the . . ."

Several of the men who'd been guarding the horses, perhaps a dozen, were beginning to mount. Jack was staring intently through the binoculars. "One of 'em's Dante," he said. "Is he gonna ride away, leave his brother and the others behind?"

"I don't think so," Clay said. "Looks to me like they're heading for that little gully. See how it cuts low, then bends around to the right of the mine? I figure they're gonna try and flank the defenders. Hit 'em from the side, get in behind 'em, bust their line."

"Yeah, yeah," Jack said. "What a chance that gives us."

Clay said nothing, only nodded. The place where the little gully rose into flatter ground would indeed take Dante's group to the extreme edge of the mine's defensive line, but it would also take the bandits very close to where Jack, Clay, and the others were hidden, within easy rifle shot. "Come on," Jack called out softly, as he ran back to the others. "Mount up."

Within a few seconds the five men were on their horses. Jack led them to one side of the rise. Just as they arrived at the lowest point, Dante and his men were coming out of the gully. Another hundred yards would put them behind the mine's defenders. "Let's hit 'em, boys," Jack said. Rifles slid from saddle scabbards. The horses were urged forward. Finally, spurs were pressed against the animals' flanks, and the five men went charging down the hill, to the right of, and slightly behind, Dante and his group.

After thirty or forty yards they had still not been spotted. Clay saw Dante raise his right arm to urge his men forward, to sweep around behind the mine defenders. Jack stood up in his stirrups, his rifle in his hands. "Hit 'em! hit 'em hard!" he shouted as he opened fire just a moment before the rest of his men.

Clay, firing quickly, saw that three or four of the men below had already been shot from their saddles. Dante's remaining men began to mill around in confusion, twisting in their saddles to stare at the five men pounding down on them. This disorder kept the bandits from putting up an effective resistance. Another three men went down, then the survivors turned their horses to race back toward the rest of the bandits.

By now Jack's men were practically among the fleeing bandits. Rifles continued to crash out. Two more of the bandits fell. Clay saw Dante trying to rally the few survivors. Clay fired at him, but missed, and now Dante, with Jack's group still killing his men, raced full out for the rest of the bandits.

Clay became aware of heavier shooting from the direction of the mine, then a lot of yelling. He turned. A dozen horsemen were pouring out from behind the mine defenses, riding toward the bandits. They'd seen unexpected help smashing into the bandits from the flank. Someone quick on the uptake had decided this was the moment to counter attack, to catch the bandits between two fires.

Jack had stopped to fire down at a fallen man who was raising a pistol. As the man was slammed back against the ground by the weight of Jack's bullet, Clay swept around to one side, angling a little to his left. "Let's get behind 'em!" he shouted to Jack and the others. Pat let out a whoop and pounded along after Clay. Tom, Jed, and Jack immediately followed.

It worked out as Clay expected. The remaining bandits, about a dozen of them, were dismounted, on fairly flat ground, firing at the approaching mine defenders. Jack's party was able to come at them from the side. Men jumped up to fire back but, under fire from two sides, began to fall. The miners, coming on, let out a shout of triumph.

The bandits were now totally demoralized. Those who could, began to run back toward where the horses were being held. The miners rode some down, firing into them as they ran. More men fell, including a couple of the miners. Some of the bandits had reached the horses and were firing back. Clay heard the smack of a bullet against flesh off to his right, heard a grunt of shock and pain. Turning, he saw that Jed had been hit, was reeling in the saddle. He looked around for the others, saw only Tom and Jack still up. Pat's horse ran by without Pat. Tom twisted in the saddle, looking for his friend, then turned and rode back.

By now the bandits were in disorganized flight. Clay saw several start to ride away, but the miners were close behind them. Two of the bandits were shot from their saddles. Four more rode away. Clay was close enough to see that Henry and Dante Duval were among them. Clay raised his rifle, fired at Dante, and again missed; the range was a hundred yards. He spurred closer. Hearing a shout from his right, he saw that Jack was riding alongside him, also firing his rifle. One of the bandits fell from his horse. Another turned back, apparently to help the man who'd fallen. Jack fired again, and the bandit flew out of his saddle. Only the two Duval brothers were left, riding into the cover of a small wood. Jack and Clay rode hard for the wood, but suddenly fire was coming their way, bullets singing past; the Duvals were firing from the cover of the trees. "Hold up!" Clay shouted to Jack . . . to ride on toward the trees was to invite a bullet. He was aware of Jack cursing in frustration as he reined his horse around. Together, he and Clay pounded back out of range, heading for the main battlefield.

They discovered that the fight was over. A number of the miners had dismounted and were walking among the fallen bandits. Clay heard a couple of shouted commands for the bandits to throw down their guns. There seemed to be no resistance at all from the bandits—they were totally broken.

Clay was surprised to see a female figure, a woman wearing long riding skirts, moving among the fallen bandits. It took him a moment to realize that it was Molly, striding from one body to another, bending down to study each man. She was carrying a light shotgun. Clay watched her straighten up from one body, could see her mouthing some words, could sense her disappointment as she started toward the next body. A chill ran through Clay. Molly was apparently searching for the bodies of the Duval brothers. What would she have done if she'd found Henry or Dante? Fire into his body with the shotgun?

Clay watched her for a moment, aware that her quest was futile—the Duvals were alive and gone. He turned as Jack rode up to him. "What are we waiting for?" Jack demanded. "They're getting away." He was pointing. Two hundred yards past the trees, two mounted figures were riding up an open slope.

Clay glanced around. There was no sign of Tom, Pat, or

Jed. Another shout from Jack, then he was spurring away, toward the two fleeing figures.

They rode through the wood without any trouble. On the far side, they saw Henry and Dante disappear over a hill. A few minutes later, Clay and Jack breasted the same hill. Jack started to spur ahead. Clay held out a hand to slow him down. "Hold up. We're gonna get bushwhacked if we just go pounding along."

Jack seemed about to continue on anyhow, but then reined up. A confused and broken landscape lay ahead—little gullies and washes, with big grassy hummocks between them—good terrain for an ambush. While they studied the landscape, Clay noticed a dark, wet area on the ground. He quickly swung down, scuffed at the stain. "Blood," he said to Jack.

"Good. One of 'em must be wounded."

"Too much blood," Clay replied. "If a man had lost this much blood . . ."

"Maybe one of their horses got hit. That should slow 'em down."

After a hasty consultation, Clay and Jack agreed that it would be best to split up and ride a hundred yards apart, each one keeping an eye on the other's back. Clay rode off to the left, while Jack headed a little to the right, following the trail of the wounded horse.

Jack was the first to come on one of the Duval brothers . . . Henry, mounted on a badly staggering horse. Jack urged his horse into a trot. Henry Duval was a hundred yards ahead. Duval heard the hoofbeats behind him, turned in the saddle, saw Jack bearing down on him. He dug his spurs into his horse's flanks. The animal managed to break into a shuffling trot, then collapsed, the front legs buckling first, then the animal fell over onto its side, pitching Henry Duval onto the ground. He hit hard, his rifle flying from his hands, spinning fifteen feet away.

Jack was upon him. As Henry struggled to get to his feet, Jack covered him with his rifle. Henry, down on one knee, looked up at Jack, his face expressionless, his eyes on the muzzle of Jack's rifle. "Guess you . . . guess you . . ." Duval croaked. He sank down onto his haunches, then looked Jack in the eyes. "Why don't you get it over with. Go ahead and shoot . . ."

To Duval's amazement, Jack slid his rifle back into its saddle scabbard, then swung down from his horse, only a dozen feet away. Duval stared at him. "I don't do things that way, Duval," Jack said. "It'd be too easy to just gun you down. No satisfaction . . ."

Hope flared in Duval's eyes. Could Kerson really be that stupid? A pistol rode in a holster on Duval's right hip. Jack jerked his head toward the pistol. "Gonna give you a chance, Duval," he said, "which is more than you've given a lot of people."

Jack stood perfectly still, his legs slightly spread, watching, as Duval, after a moment's hesitation, got to his feet. Duval was careful to keep his hand away from the butt of his pistol until he was fully erect, facing Jack. Both men stood quietly for half a minute. Neither felt there was anything more to be said. They both crouched a little, their right hands sliding toward the butts of their pistols.

At that moment Clay was a hundred yards away. He had been following a set of tracks. He knew that Jack was on the trail of whoever was riding the wounded horse, which meant the man ahead of him was probably riding a healthy animal. So Clay proceeded cautiously. He rode along a wash, with hummocks rising up on each side. He carefully scanned the terrain ahead and to either side, looking for signs of a man waiting in ambush.

To his surprise, the tracks he was following began to curve around to the right. He could see that from the tracks the horse was moving at a quick trot. Clay followed quickly.

Looking ahead, he saw that a gully would force the rider to bear even more to the right, until he'd be heading back toward the point where Clay had first spotted the pool of blood. Clay saw that he could cut the circle the rider was following, perhaps take him from the side.

An especially high mound of grassy dirt rose up a bit to the right. Clay thought he saw movement high up on its left side, caught sight of something long and dark, perhaps the barrel of a rifle. He swung down from his horse, then jogged forward, rifle in hand, the soft earth muffling the sound of his running.

As Clay came out from behind a clump of brush, he saw, off to his right, maybe fifty yards away, Jack Kerson and Henry Duval facing one another, both men standing tense, ready to kill.

To the left, and high up, half-hidden behind the summit of the mound, Clay saw Dante Duval, with his rifle pointing down toward Jack, ready to shoot him in the back.

There was no time to shout, no time to warn Jack. Instead, Clay raised his rifle, aimed for a fraction of a second, then fired at Dante.

Clay was able to see two things happen—Dante fell back, the rifle falling from his grasp, and at the same moment, Henry Duval and Jack Kerson, both galvanized into action by the sound of Clay's shot, reached for their pistols.

Clay was surprised by how fast Henry was; his gun was out of its holster a fraction of a second before Jack's and Henry got off the first shot, standing half-crouched as the pistol in his hand belched white smoke.

Jack stayed erect, apparently unhit, his pistol held out in front of him. Taking his time, he fired once, twice, both bullets slamming Henry Duval backward.

Clay jerked his eyes away from Henry Duval and Jack Kerson, because a pistol boomed forty yards in front of him. He had a glimpse of Dante's face behind a bloom of gunsmoke. Dante's mouth was twisted into a rictus of hatred, his shout lost in the sound of the shot.

Clay jumped to his right as Dante's bullet winged past where he'd been standing. Clay rolled when he hit, but his rifle, caught beneath him, was torn from his grasp.

He had to get under cover. So he sprinted forward, heading for the base of the mound, while reaching for his pistol. He had been peering toward the left side of the mound, searching for Dante, when he became aware of a shower of dirt cascading downward. It took him a split second to realize that Dante must have slipped all the way around the mound . . . then . . . awareness of a dark shape falling toward him, Dante launching himself from the mound, straight at Clay.

Clay had time to take half a step to the right, which kept his body from absorbing Dante's full weight. While he managed to stay on his feet, he could not keep from dropping his pistol.

Then he was grappling with Dante, who seized him by the throat with his left hand, while clawing for his pistol with the other. Clay tensed his neck muscles to keep Dante's thumb from digging into his windpipe, then raised his left arm, making a desperate grasp for Dante's gun hand. He succeeded in catching him by the wrist. Dante had managed to pull his pistol free of its holster, and was holding the pistol pointed upward, trying to cock it while Clay forced the hand up and back, moving the muzzle away from his head.

They stood locked in a wordless struggle for several seconds. Dante's left hand was still locked around Clay's throat, while he tried to force his right hand back down, to bring the muzzle of his pistol to bear on Clay's head. There were grunts, gasps for air, the two men straining against one another.

Clay sensed that he was losing the contest. Dante had shut off too much of his air; spots were forming in front of Clay's eyes. Dante's gun hand began to press further and further down. He'd managed to get the pistol cocked.

Clay's right hand had been clawing at the hand locked on

his throat. He suddenly let go, could see the look of triumph on Dante's face, but Clay had not given up the fight, had simply changed tactics. Reaching across his body with his right hand, his fingers closed around the handle of his big bowie knife. "You're dead, Parker," he heard Dante snarl.

Then the snarl changed to a hideous sound that was half-grunt, half-scream as Clay jerked the bowie from its sheath, then sank the razor sharp blade into Dante's abdomen. Clay became aware that Dante's hand was no longer at his throat, and that the pistol seemed to be slipping from Dante's grip.

The two men remained standing close together for several more seconds. Then Dante's pistol thudded onto the ground. Clay moved back two steps, standing clear, still wary. Dante's eyes remained on Clay's for several more seconds, then Dante lowered his head, looked down at the knife handle sticking out of his body. "God," he grunted, staring at the blood coursing down his body. Then again, his voice low but clear . . . "God."

He began to go down, very slowly, falling first to his knees. Clay saw Dante's eyes lose focus, then glaze over. A moment later he pitched forward onto his face.

Clay became aware of movement off to his right. He whirled toward where he had dropped his pistol, then saw Jack, standing a few yards away and staring at Dante, at the huge pool of blood around him.

Clay glanced away, half aware that Jack was saying, "Henry's dead."

Clay nodded, then went over and picked up his pistol, using his left hand so that he wouldn't get Dante's blood all over it. He had a difficult time getting the pistol back into the holster. He went over to Dante's body. He had to put his foot on Dante's chest before he was able to pull out his knife. He walked over to where a small stream ran out from between two rocks. Kneeling, he carefully washed, first the knife, then his right arm. There was too much blood. He pulled off his shirt, and dumped it in the water, which quickly turned red.

When he straightened up, Jack was bringing their horses. Clay dug a dry shirt out of his saddle bags and put it on. Jack had found his rifle; Clay saw that it was once again in its saddle scabbard. Both men mounted. Jack looked over to where he'd killed Henry Duval, then to Dante's body. He shook his head. "Let somebody else bury them."

Jack pulled his horse around. "Gotta get back and see how Pat and Tom are. I think Jed got hit."

Clay nodded.

"Then I'm gonna ride on out of here," Jack continued. "Catch up to Uncle Tod and the wagon, ride on back to Los Angeles with Luke."

Another nod from Clay, but he did not turn his horse.

"Come with us," Jack said. "You'll like Los Angeles."

Clay shook his head. He had no intention of heading back toward the mine . . . the sight of Molly roaming the battle-field with her shotgun like an avenging fury . . .

"I appreciate the offer," he said to Jack, "but I figure it's time to head off on my own."

"Where to?" Jack asked.

For the first time Clay smiled. "Kinda thinking about San Francisco."

Jack looked surprised. "Any particular reason?"

"Figure on taking a look at some hats," Clay replied. "Fancy hats. Women's hats."

Jack grinned, nodded. He turned his horse and rode away. Clay sat his horse quietly until Jack had disappeared from sight. Only then did he urge his own horse into motion, turn-ing the animal in a direction that would take him wide of the mine, wide of the site of the fight and wide of the town.

As he rode, his mind formed an image of a small shop high on one of San Francisco's hills, maybe with a view over the bay. In that shop, among the hats and scarves, there was a woman with dark hair and eyes. A woman who did not hate.